PRAISE FOR JANE MENDELSOHN'S

Innocence

A *St. Louis Post-Dispatch* Best Book of the Year

"Remarkable . . . Mendelsohn's writing, which manages to perfectly capture the poetic and slightly overblown sensibilities of a teenager filled with self-loathing and *weltschmertz*, lulls the reader into believing that this will be your everyday peep into the mind of tormented youth. . . . Then, slowly, almost imperceptibly, the novel undergoes a metamorphosis. A struggle of mythic, medieval proportions emerges from behind the facade of everyday life. . . . Add Mendelsohn's atmospheric writing and creepy, foreboding imagery to a terrific plot, and the result is a truly thrilling read."
—*Newsday*

"Beckett's perceptions about what's going on around her simply make literal the psychic terrors and traumas of modern teenage life. Like Gregor Samsa in Kafka's *Metamorphosis*, who awakes one morning to find himself transformed into a giant dung beetle—a literal embodiment of his predicament as a cog in the wheel of industrial capitalism—Beckett assumes the role of a slasher-flick heroine because in a sense she has been one all along."
—*The Denver Post*

"If Beckett Warner, our desperate, likable protagonist, seems frozen somewhere between *Revenge of the Vampire Sluts* and *Catcher in the Rye*, that's because the world she's grown up in is beholden to both. . . . Laconic and edgy and begrudgingly tragic . . . the novel is onto itself as well as the formulas it exposes, offering a darkly appealing glance at popular culture and modern urban mayhem. Like Jeffrey Eugenedies's *The Virgin Suicides* and Jay McInerney's *Bright Lights, Big City*, Mendelsohn's story muffles its death and sorrow in terminal irony, though the trait is less irritating than it might be because *Innocence* doesn't try to be more than it is. Following in the footsteps of all the Final Girls who have gone before— 'Persephone, Dorothy, Lolita,' Beckett tells us—this heroine, too, tries to find her way back home. But her yellow brick road is more redolent of subway tunnel than flower-strewn path; in *Innocence*, there's nary a munchkin in sight."
—*The Boston Sunday Globe*

"A wild, unsettling but tightly-crafted flight through the world of a teenage New Yorker that blends allegorical gothic horror with realistic coming-of-age angst with culturally savvy media-like sound bites and blurs of reality and fantasy. . . . *Innocence* becomes a wild ride into the experience of stripping away all fears, dictums, and reflections and finally facing the self in its isolated pure strength. It's a ride with Alice down the rabbit hole. It's furious Carrie and the robotic Stepford Wives meet Dracula. But in the end it's also Germaine Greer . . . "
—*The Providence Sunday Journal*

"[Mendelsohn] cooks up a strew of paranoia and gothic fantasy that makes for a suprisingly unique mystery novel. Told in spare, melodramatic vignettes, the book has elements of both an epic poem and horror films." —*Time Out New York*

"Sleek prose and a chilling, affectless tone shape this noirish modern-gothic coming-of-age story . . . In homage to *Heathers* as well as Hitchcock . . . invoking classic tropes in horror films, Mendelsohn constructs a twisted world in which innocence has somehow become a disease, and adolescent fancies spiral into dark realities. There's a surprisingly upbeat ending to this smart allegory as Mendelsohn suggests that the reintegration of the self can triumph over the emotional turmoil of coming-of-age." —*Publishers Weekly*

"[A] scary, tricky neo-gothic thriller . . . Invoking a battery of analogues favoring the pop-culture heroines of *Alice in Wonderland*, *The Wizard of Oz*, and *Lolita*, Mendelsohn isolates her plucky heroine so fearfully via sparse paragraphs and an underpeopled world that even the most preposterous threats leap out of the movie frame to fuel a shriek of pure paranoia. . . . Must-reading for anybody who thinks teenagers today have gotten bloated with entitlement: a scarlet will-o'-the-wisp fantasy in which adults and adulthood aren't stupid stiffs but agents of unimaginable evil." —*Kirkus Reviews*

"Bizarre, compelling, surprising, horrific . . . If you locked up Judy Blume, Sylvia Plath and Anne Rice in a room together and forced them to collaborate. . . . If you were to envision the book as a movie, *Innocence* would be *Rosemary's Baby*, *Interview with the Vampire*, and *The Virgin Suicides* rolled into one. *Innocence* flies like a bat out of the hell that is middle school. Beyond the blood and terror, the book is a legitimate, albeit dark, social commentary on the contemporary American teenager." —*Intelligencer Journal* (Lancaster, PA)

innocence

jane mendelsohn

RIVERHEAD BOOKS

NEW YORK

RIVERHEAD BOOKS
Published by The Berkley Publishing Group
A division of Penguin Putnam Inc.
375 Hudson Street
New York, New York 10014

For the concept of the Final Girl, the author is indebted to *Men, Women, and Chainsaws:
Gender in the Modern Horror Film*, by Carol J. Clover (Princeton University Press, 1992).

Copyright © 2000 by Jane Mendelsohn
Book design by Marysarah Quinn
Cover design by Honi Werner
Cover art based on photograph by Juan Silva/TIB

Published simultaneously in Canada.

First Riverhead hardcover edition: August 2000
First Riverhead trade paperback edition: May 2001
Riverhead trade paperback ISBN: 1-57322-874-5

The Penguin Putnam Inc. World Wide Web site address is
www.penguinputnam.com

The Library of Congress has catalogued the Riverhead hardcover edition as follows:

Mendelsohn, Jane.
Innocence : a novel / by Jane Mendelsohn.
p.   cm.
ISBN 1-57322-164-3
1. Teenage girls—Fiction.   2. Stepmothers—Fiction.
3. Vampires—Fiction.   I. Title.
PS3563.E482 156   2000   00-032839
813'.54—dc21

PRINTED IN THE UNITED STATES OF AMERICA

10   9   8   7   6   5   4   3   2

for NPD

It wasn't a dream.

I come to the park to remember. Around me, the city melts. It dissolves like a black-and-white reflection on the surface of the water.

Here, everything is color. The grass a stained-glass green. The blue between the leaves. Visions and voices escape from my mind like butterflies up into the trees.

There's nothing to be afraid of.

Soaring with bats over the electric city. Diving into the darkness past liquid ribbons of light. The silver buildings seen from up above, silent tombstones in the early morning.

My name is Beckett, and this is not a dream. This is not a delusion. This is not based on a true story. This is true.

Doesn't anyone believe me?

part one

1

THEY WERE ALL DEAD. I WAS THE ONLY
one left.

They'd done something awful with a pink plastic razor, two of
them on the bed and one on the floor. The music was still lapping on the CD player. I think I mouthed the words.

Outside, it was one of those sunsets that nobody looks at, a red
and orange and purple massacre, spilling its guts out above
the city.

I don't understand why nobody notices. Those sunsets,
they bleed all over.

. . .

I ran. I ran as fast as I could through the park as the sun set. First the sky turned gray, like smudged newsprint—there seemed to be words up there—and then it all faded to blue. The leaves on the trees went from green to purple. The street lamps turned on. As I ran out of the park behind the museum, night fell. I could hear it. Everything became quieter. The cabs stopped honking and slid by with their secret passengers. Lights arrived in the buildings like stars. Traffic moved in one wave downtown. It was Friday night. The sky went black as a limousine.

Why was I running? I was running from images: a sneaker, a mirror, two words. I remember blood hanging in strings off the bottom of a shoe like gum. I remember two words scrawled across a mirror.

Two words: *Drink Me.*

I ran. I ran past the front of the museum where the fountains glowed green from their swimming-pool lights. On the steps of the museum, a group of kids. I ran across Fifth Avenue. A bus pulled by and stopped, and heaved like an old accordion. I turned onto a street and then down Park Avenue through the dark canyon of buildings. Behind me I felt the presence of someone, something, but I knew I couldn't turn around or stop. That's when it started raining. I let the rain drip through my hair and down the ends of it, onto my shirt. My sneakers filled with water. It was raining so hard I could have missed the building, but I stopped out of instinct. At first, the doorman didn't want to let me up without buzzing. But I flirted a little. I let him stare at my shirt.

Upstairs, outside the elevator, I dug my fingers into the dirt of the plant. I found the key. I slipped into the apartment. I could tell by the quiet that Tobey's parents were out, and I followed the sound of the television to his room. He was watching an old movie. Voices crying across time. I followed the blue light.

The blue light cast a glow over his sleeping face. Raindrops slid down the walls like tears. I looked at him, at his innocent face. He must have felt my presence, my fear. He woke up.

Beckett, he said with his eyes, what are you doing here?

I took off my T-shirt. I dropped it on the floor.

Then I said: Fuck me.

2

HOW CAN I GET YOU TO BELIEVE ME, TO believe the unbelievable? I want so much for you to understand. But you can't make someone believe you. Trust is a secret combination to a lock. Two turns of faith, one turn of fantasy, half a turn of truth. *Trust me.* It sounds so false.

What if I tell you that I'm still running? I'm running and remembering. Branches cut my legs, wet leaves stick to my clothes, and memories tangle in my hair. I'm running through a park, and then a city, and then a building. I hear strange languages, words of despair. The things I see along the way frighten me, but I can't look away.

. . .

Persephone, Dorothy, Lolita, the Final Girl, all went down to Hell. Persephone, Dorothy, Lolita, the Final Girl: I'm following you. Wait for me.

3

GREAT HEROINES HAVE DEAD MOTHERS.
That's what I told myself when she died. After she died (highway, drunk driver), my father decided that we should move
back to the city. He took an apartment on the Upper West Side
and enrolled me in a fancy school. I remember the first day, my
terror.

I was scared when I walked into the cafeteria, the talking, the
groups of friends. I walked into the cafeteria and saw them,
mermaids washed up on shore. I saw the girls in their wide-
legged jeans, the thin strings around their wrists, and I felt
frightened. Their hair swung down like rope. I watched the
boys sharing headphones; I studied their glances, the T-shirts
covered with writing, their eyelashes, the muscles on their arms.

. . .

There I am, sitting alone. I'm the ugly girl, the smart girl, the boyish girl, the loser. I'm the one who knows too much.

I sat listening while I stared intently at my lunch. I was listening to the beautiful girls. Their names were Sunday, Morgan, and Myrrh. Every now and then I looked up through my stringy hair and watched them talking. Nobody looked at me.

You know that girl I was talking about? Sunday said.

Yeah, just a minute ago?

Yeah. Well, apparently, when she went down on him she forgot that she was chewing gum.

You're kidding.

No, I'm not.

That's hysterical.

It was a total mess.

The mermaids laughed in catty euphoria. The thunder of the lunchroom rose up behind them.

I'd like to tell you that I was better than they were, that they were dead souls, lost girls, superficial. But I wanted nothing more than to be like them. I wanted hair that swung down like rope.

. . .

This is what's happening: I'm running away. Away from these memories, away from myself. But the faster I run, the faster they follow me, until they're ahead of me and I'm running into them. I run into them like a girl stepping inside the movie screen. I run into them, and my world turns from black-and-white to color.

I run straight inside my eye. It's ten feet tall.

He walked into the cafeteria with his hands in his pockets and the strap of his bag across the front of his chest like a sash. The cafeteria was noisy and the tables were full and the women behind the food counter were wearing hair nets and bending over and scooping tuna fish out with ice cream scoops. He stood on line, accepted what they offered, and then walked slowly in my direction to the table with the beautiful girls. He laid down his tray and nodded and lifted the strap over his head and set his bag down gently on a seat. He sat down and put his elbows on the table and leaned forward and smiled with his eyes.

Sunday stuck out her arm in front of his face.

Smell my perfume. Isn't it amazing?

Yeah, amazing. He took a swig of soda.

Who's your friend?

Sunday shook her hair out behind her and pulled her knees up to rest against the table.

Why don't you find out? she said.

He took a bite of food and a long sip of soda.

You guys are friendly, he said. Then, showing them how it's done: I'm Tobey. What's your name?

I lifted my eyes. My face went hot, a stick of cartoon dynamite exploding inside my head.

Beckett.

I heard the girls laugh under their breath.

Hi, Beckett. This is Sunday, Morgan, and Myrrh.

The three girls glanced at me, nodded, and glanced away. He was enjoying playing the adult.

Where you from? What school?

You wouldn't know it, it's far away.

He waited for more.

Long Island. Way out on the North Fork.

He nodded and took another mouthful of food. Sunday squirmed in her seat and lowered her eyelids. Myrrh was wearing a wool cap and a tank top with her bra straps showing, and she stood up and walked over behind Sunday and started playing with Sunday's hair.

I took a deep breath.

Myrrh, I said. That's a cool name. How did you get it?

Parents were hippies.

Used to be.

Now they just buy a lot of CDs.

Sunday shook her hair.

Wow, Tobey said. What insight. You guys are so ironic and self-aware.

Oh, please, said Morgan.

I have to go, said Myrrh.

Sunday left without saying anything.

Oh, well, he said. I guess it's just us.

I could have watched the smooth human machinery of his hands all day. But I picked up my tray and my book bag and left.

4

THERE'S A CHARACTER IN EVERY HORROR movie who doesn't die. She's the survivor, the Final Girl. She's the one who finds the bodies of her friends and understands that she is in danger. She is the one who runs and suffers. She is the one who shrieks and falls. Her friends understand what is happening to them for no more than an instant before they are killed. But the Final Girl knows for hours, maybe days, that she is going to die. She feels death coming. She hears it. She sees it.

Welcome to my nightmare.

5

I WAS LOOKING OUT THE WINDOW. IT WAS AFTER-
noon. The clouds had softened and blurred to X rays, a thousand shades of gray. I turned away. The door to the classroom
was open, and I saw someone walk past. It looked like Tobey.

I raised my hand. I was excused.

In the nurse's office, a kid in a chair with a thermometer in
his mouth. The nurse had her back to the kid when Tobey
walked in.

He looked at the kid, and said, Nurse, I think you've made
a mistake.

What kind of mistake?

He winked at the kid, and said, I believe this is a rectal
thermometer.

Tobey, get out of here.

But I feel sick.

You are sick.

Excuse me, I said from the doorway.

Oh, you again, he said. He smiled.

The nurse turned around and looked at me.

Can I help you? she said.

I don't feel well.

She's new, Tobey said.

What's your name?

Beckett, Tobey and I said at the same time.

Why don't we have a look at you, Beckett?

I sat down on a low chair.

What seems to be the matter?

I have an earache, I said.

The nurse put her soft hand on my forehead. As she did that, she took the thermometer out of the kid's mouth and said, You can go back to class now.

Then Tobey said, We're all sick around here.

Oh, come on, she said, it's not that bad, is it?

When she turns to me, it seems to happen in slow motion. First her hair moves, then her eyes, then her mouth. She looks like a movie star playing a nurse. She has dark red hair and green eyes.

. . .

She picked up one of those instruments with a light and a little funnel at one end. She inserted it into my ear while Tobey watched and I blushed and shut my eyelids. I heard the ocean.

It looks fine in there.

She stuck a thermometer in my mouth. I felt the cold wet needle of it under my tongue.

I looked at Tobey with my lips pursed.

Give it a couple of months, she'll be like everyone else, he said.

What do you mean by that? said the nurse, raising her eyebrow.

You know what I mean. There's a curse on this place. People keep killing themselves.

The nurse shot him a glance. She took an index card out of a box and wrote my name on it. I liked the look of my name in her handwriting.

She wrote "general malaise" down on the index card.

Come on, he said. You know what I'm talking about.

His hair fell into his eyes. He tossed it back. Then he said, Last year a bunch of girls, very hot girls, I might add, made a suicide pact and kept it.

The nurse took the thermometer out of my mouth.

But I can't blame them, he said. Life sucks and then you die, right?

Tobey, get out of here.

I'm going. I'm going.

Ninety-eight point six, she said. Perfectly normal.

That night I heard the voices of the beautiful girls. They rose up from the floor and whispered from the walls. They said my name: Beckett. They told me not to trust the nurse. They told me she hated them because they were young and pretty. I told them, But she's young and pretty, too. That made them laugh. Then the nurse appeared in my dream. She was crouching, digging in the soil. She wore a white trench coat and white spike-heel shoes. Behind her, red and yellow flowers and bright green leaves made a backdrop, a Technicolor garden. The nurse was looking up, as if she were afraid someone might see her. Her hair fell over one eye. Her dark eyebrows knit together with worry like two black ink lines in a Japanese comic strip. Her lips were red. She was digging up a dead body.

Then the nurse became a bat and then a hundred bats. Then a million, winging up to the sky in a dark funnel like a cyclone. The bats escaped into the sky to the sound of the girls' voices: whispers and laughter and my name.

This might seem like a terrifying experience, but it wasn't. It was just a dream, and the voices were only words.

6

MY FATHER WAS IN THE KITCHEN WHEN I GOT
home. He was making something for dinner. Beckett? he called.

I walked into the doorway. He was wearing an apron and
had some tomato sauce on his shirt.

So, he said, who said what to whom?

I walked over to the refrigerator and took out an apple.

Nobody said anything to me.

It'll take a while.

I suppose so.

He threw in the spaghetti.

Then he said, It's Friday night. You free for a date?

I bit the apple. He looked so eager.

Sure, I said.

Okay, then. Let's do it. His eyes were staring hard at me.
You pick the flick.

. . .

After she died, my father put a cot in my room and slept on it for two weeks. He said he was worried about me. Every night I heard him lying awake. A whispering, muttering sadness.

During the movie I turned around and watched the picture beam from the projector. It sliced through the darkened room like a ray of sunlight underwater. People's faces flickered as if deep-sea vegetation were waving back and forth in front of them.

My father stretched out his arm around my shoulders, but I squirmed away.

I like to watch a movie reflected in the faces of the audience. I see the story like a dream fluttering in their eyes.

In the restroom the lights seemed to be searchlights. I had to squint. I was surprised to see my face in the mirror. It was my usual ugly face, but I was happy to see it. After looking at those giant faces for two hours, I was relieved to see my plain ugly face and stringy hair. Everyone else around me, though, I felt them pushing me out of the way to get to the mirror. The mirror was the most popular person in the room.

. . .

I picture us walking home, my father's aggressively normal face, a mask of cheerfulness, comfort, and concern, and my own, a little too absorbed in my ice cream, and I think: No one watching would notice anything unusual. We look perfectly normal.

When we turned the corner, we saw the police car pulled up to the curb, and the crowd of people. My father's face reddened on and off with the flashing lights. An ambulance approached from the other direction.

They're in the alley, one cop said.

How many?

Three of them. A dog walker found them.

The crowd opened up to let the paramedics through. I could see in an alley, past a Dumpster, an outstretched hand. I moved around the outside of the crowd and walked up the steps of a brownstone, where I could look over and see into the alley. A drop of ice cream fell onto my sneaker.

In the alley, three girls were stretched out on the ground. Mermaids washed up on shore. Their hair fanned out around them, and their legs seemed to float on the surface of a pool of blood. They looked like refugees from a beach party, their limbs akimbo like dancers'. One of them was wearing a long skirt hiked up over her thighs, and the two others had on jeans that were soaked through, black with blood.

For a moment, they looked real, and then the next thing I knew, they were imprisoned in a gruesome photograph in my mind.

I watched the paramedics lift the bodies onto stretchers until my father found me and took my arm.

I know them, I said.

They're friends of yours?

No. I know them from school. Should I tell the police?

7

EVERYONE WENT TO THE MEMORIAL SER-
vice. The girls wore black skirts and just a little jewelry, their
mothers wore suits and more jewelry. The boys shrugged their
widening shoulders inside their jackets and kept their hands in
their pockets. Their ties swung like leashes.

Inside, three coffins were covered with flowers, stuffed ani-
mals, yearbooks, CDs, homemade signs, collages, snapshots,
and one wool hat. I squeezed my father's hand as we walked by.
I heard a car alarm go off inside my head. I remembered my
mother's funeral. The silence in my heart. A tree weeping on
the road. I remembered the girls and their long, lovely hair. I
wanted to pull out my hair.

. . .

A group of girls sang a song about friendship that I'd heard on the radio. One woman gave a long speech. She talked about the pressures on teenagers. When she got to the podium, she took her glasses out of their case and put them on. I wondered why she couldn't have done that earlier. There were smudges around her eyes, soft black rings of mascara that made her irises appear more blue. I had the feeling that she liked the look of tear-smudged mascara.

Across the room, I caught sight of Tobey. I saw him slide down in his seat and put on his sunglasses.

What have we done? What can we do? These are the questions that we must look inside to answer.

I realized that the woman speaking was his mother.

After the service, mothers stood on the sidewalk talking to one another while teary students exchanged hugs. My father and I walked out into the brightness, and for a few moments we just stood there, with no one to talk to. Then I saw her. Under a dark red awning halfway down the block, a woman in a short leather coat was looking at us. Her hair lifting, lifting higher at the touch of the wind. She took off her sunglasses and shaded her eyes with her hands as if she were spotting land out at sea. Putting her sunglasses back on and slipping them up to rest on her head, she smiled at me, and started walking toward us.

Who is that woman? my father asked.

She's the school nurse, I said.

She walked up to us and greeted me. She held out her hand to my father. On the sidewalk, three women with rigid smiles turned around to watch her.

You must be Beckett's father.

You must be the school nurse.

How can you tell?

The white uniform. No, Beckett told me.

They smiled.

Miles Warner.

Pamela Reeve.

Then she said, It's terrible about the girls.

Awful. Just awful. I'm very concerned.

I'm sure. Did you know it happened last year?

I heard that.

We did a lot of counseling, but I guess we didn't do enough.

The three of us stood in silence for a while. People trafficked around us, discussing logistics and leaving in awkward groups.

Then she asked me how I was doing. She said it was

hard to be new. My father said that's what he kept telling me.

But he wasn't looking at me. He was looking at her.

I wanted my father to meet the nurse. I wanted someone else
to take care of him. But it occurred to me on the sidewalk that
I'd made a terrible mistake. I wanted him back. I wanted him
all to myself. At night I heard these sirens in my head.

8

HE FELL IN LOVE WITH THE SCHOOL nurse. Their entire courtship, which took about fifteen minutes, felt like one of those montage sequences where the hero and heroine go to street fairs and walk on the beach and have candlelit dinners and get caught in the rain.

Later, it made sense. They were in a commercial for love. And what they were selling was me.

They must have both felt that they were doing the right thing. Everyone thinks they're doing the right thing. But some people can't see anyone but themselves. They think they can, but they're always looking in a mirror. They think they're doing the right thing for someone else, but that someone else turns out to be themselves.

. . .

We went to her apartment for dinner. I don't know why they didn't just go on a date, the two of them, but I guess they needed to pretend that they were getting together for my benefit, to help me fit in at school.

She lived in a white brick building that took up half a block. It was downtown, at a busy intersection where you could feel the vibration of the subway pulsing up through the sidewalk and hear the buses choking when they stopped at the corner. Inside, the building had an empty lobby with empty chairs and a doorman behind a fake-looking desk. The elevator was plain, with dim lights, and the hallways were carpeted but shabby and very long, like the corridors in a hotel. I kept thinking somebody would emerge from behind one of the doors, but nobody did. Then I thought maybe no one lived behind them at all.

Her apartment was small. It was practically empty, and she had only the necessities: a table, four chairs, a low couch, and a coffee table. She didn't have a clock, or a plant. In the bedroom she had a bed and a little rug.

After dinner I went and sat on her bed, and she took out a little TV from the closet and plugged it in, but I could hear them talking in the next room.

You don't have much furniture, he said.

I know. I'm not into decorating. Some people think it seems monastic.

No, not at all. I like it. It's sort of, um, conceptual.

Her laughter pulled you in, like her eyes.

Beckett tells me you're a writer.

Guilty as charged.

What do you write?

Novels, travel books, magazine pieces.

You should come to my book group. We'd love to have a real writer.

I'd like that.

I watched television for a while, and then:

Do you like working at the school?

Yes, but it's just a day job. I'm a student myself.

Oh really. What are you studying?

Transpersonal psychology and brainwave biofeedback.

That's a mouthful.

It's very interesting.

She got up and walked someplace, probably into the kitchen, and I couldn't make out anything more.

I fell asleep. In my sleep I dreamed about my father and Pamela on the TV show I had been watching. One of those lame teen horror shows where the girls all wear lipstick and the scariest thing is how skinny everyone is. When I opened my eyes, my father was standing in the bedroom.

Hey, kiddo, looks like you fell asleep, he said. His tie was

loose, and he was smoking a cigarette. He smoked three cigarettes a year.

She'd walked in behind him. Her cheeks were flushed. She
was holding a glass of red wine.

He looked at his watch. It's getting late, he said. And you
have school tomorrow. He smiled at her. Both of you.

She stood in the doorway while we waited for the elevator.

Thanks for coming, she said.

Sometimes I picture an elevator hurtling down, ripped loose
from its black cables. I picture the metal box falling like a piece
of a planet, a meteor smacking the earth. I hear the concussion
of steel against steel. I see sparks zapping all over like the
thoughts of a mad genius. It doesn't scare me at all.

9

IT DIDN'T TAKE LONG FOR US TO BECOME
a kind of family, me, my father, and Pamela. *Pamela,* I called her
that now when we weren't in school.

We went to the movies and on picnics. She brought me pre-
sents. One day she gave me a kitten. I stroked the kitten's back
and felt the bones beneath her skin. The little skeleton reminded me of my mother's hands. Then the kitten opened her
eyes very slowly, lifting her lids part-way, and seemed to be
happy and despairing at the same time.

What are you thinking? I said to the kitten.

That was when she bit me.

. . .

My father, Pamela, and I ate lunch and then walked along the bike path, the skaters swerving past us as they slid downhill.

When she takes off her sunglasses and puts them on top of her head, I watch how she does it. I want to be like her.

We ate under a tree.

What have you got up your sleeve next? Pamela asked. Champagne?

I have a bottle cooling in the boat pond.

At the boat pond the light splashed across the water like confetti. We took a boat out.

Do you really have a bottle of champagne out here? I asked.

I wanted to die when they both laughed. I ran my fingers across the sparkling pond.

The sparkles separated and showed the murky water.

You ready for canoeing next weekend? my father asked.

I looked up. Where are we going?

My father looked at her. Pamela looked at him. I pushed my hair out of my eyes with wet fingers.

Actually, my father said, Pamela and I are going away next weekend. He looked back at her.

My school is having a retreat, Pamela said.

Pamela pulled her sunglasses down from her head and put them on.

My father squinted. It's just for the weekend.

He paddled a little faster as the light slid sideways. There were shadows under his eyes.

We don't have to go, Pamela said.

Beckett will be fine. Won't you?

The light on the pond was darker now. Green-sequined skirts rustling across a dance floor. Her eyes were green, green like the water.

Miles, she said, when we got out of the boat.

I didn't even listen to the rest.

1 0

I LOOKED AT HER LEATHER COAT AND
then up at her. She was the last person in the world I wanted
to see.

She said she had homework too. A paper for her psychology class. She wanted my father to read it.

Is anything the matter? she asked.

Why?

I was wondering why you haven't been coming by my
office to visit.

I've just been busy.

Cat came into the room and nuzzled her face into Pamela's
leg.

Maybe you're blue because you have your period?

She picked up the kitten and put her in her lap.

I blushed again. I don't have my period, I said.

Are you premenstrual?

I turned and looked at my desk. I haven't gotten it yet, I said.

Don't worry, she said. You will.

Who's that guy in the poster? He's cute.

Kurt Cobain.

She stared at the poster. Kurt had black eyeliner around his eyes.

It's from a movie. Jen got it for me.

Cat jumped off of her lap.

You spending more time with Jen?

She's pretty much my only friend.

I thought we were friends.

She looked at me really hard. Her eyes were like tunnels.

She gave me one more present. It was a bottle of perfume. I never wore perfume. Thanks, I said.

I guess I looked like I didn't know what to do with it, so she took it from me and spritzed some in the air.

I sniffed. Cat sniffed. Then I sneezed. Pamela and I laughed.

She took my hand and sprayed some on my wrist. I felt the cool wet stain on my skin.

That's when my father walked in.

What are you two up to?

Girl talk.

Pamela gave me some perfume.

He pretended to smell it. Smells good. He smiled.

For a second it felt as if all three of us were really there, together. In the night, three people, a warmth, a kind of family. Then he pointed to the papers in his hand, and he said, Listen, this is terrific. I just have a couple of constructive criticisms.

She looked up at him. I can't wait to hear them, she said.

Good night, we all said.

After she left, I put the bottle of perfume on my dresser.

Then I went to the bathroom and washed it off.

1 1

THE DREAMS GOT WORSE, DARKENED, went up in flames. The heat of the projector burning through the film, igniting the images, melting the screen. The negative of my mind shriveling at the seams.

Sitting at the end of my bed was Sunday, one of the beautiful girls. Her hair was dripping wet with blood.

Would you comb my hair for me, Beckett? She reached out her arm and handed me a comb. I'm having so much trouble. It's all tangled.

She smiled at me like I was her friend. I took the comb.

The problem is, it's all wet. I can't seem to get it dry. She took a hunk of her hair and twisted it until the blood squeezed out, onto the bed. See?

She turned her body to the side while I sat next to her on the bed. I started combing her long, wet hair. When I was finished and it was all untangled, she turned around and said, Let me do yours.

As the comb slid through my stringy hair, I felt a wet sensation on my scalp. You really should use a different conditioner, she said.

She kept combing my hair with the bloody comb. She sang a song that I recognized from the radio. The comb slid down my scalp and scraped my neck like nails.

1 2

IN CLASS, THE TEACHER SAID SOMETHING about the unreliable narrator. The unreliable narrator was a device. A device for what? For creating ironic distance, she said. Oh, said Tobey. So you mean, like, it's okay to lie.

No, it's not lying. It's a literary technique.

Cool. I had sex with every girl in this school.

That's a lie, another kid said.

No, it's not, Tobey said. I'm just an unreliable narrator.

Music flew by me. Heavenly, dark, lyrical music glided past me, and I followed it. It swerved into song and then out of song; someone sang, and then the music swallowed them up. It throbbed and sank and bottomed out and lifted. I walked up some stairs that led to the auditorium. Inside, a group of boys was practicing. They wore T-shirts with the word Suck. After a while—I guess they had to go to class—they stopped and put away their instruments. I watched them carry their guitars as they picked up their jackets and knapsacks—they carried them so gently—and then I watched them as they jumped down softly from the stage.

I knew then that I wanted to be up there one day, singing, but I didn't have a voice. It seemed to me that it could never happen. I could never stand onstage and open my mouth and watch butterflies pour out of it.

Later, I told Dr. Kent about the butterflies. She asked me what they meant to me, if they had anything to do with the bats. I said the bats were butterflies that had lost their innocence. Then I said, Are you going to put that in your book?

13

THERE WAS A BOUQUET OF FLOWERS IN MY room. I had this weird thought that they were from my mother: *Just thinking of you.* My father had put the flowers in water, and they spilled out of a vase and filled the room with a fruity scent. A tiny white envelope lay hidden among the petals and leaves. I saw it when I leaned forward to drink in the smell. The petals touched my cheeks like babies' hands, cool and moist, and I surrendered to their curiosity. The roses brushed against my cheeks. The irises worked their way into my hair.

To my best girl, the note said.

Do you like them? He was standing in the doorway.

They're really pretty, I said.

He came in and sat down on the bed. He ran his fingers through his hair. Look, he said, I know I've been busy lately, with my work and, I'll admit it, with Pamela. But I want you to know that I'm always here for you.

Where is she?

She's at her book group.

Why didn't you go?

I haven't read the book. I thought we'd have a special dinner alone tonight. Just you and me.

I guess I looked surprised.

What do you say, a special night, just the two of us?

It was growing dark and the lights were off and his face was disintegrating in the shadows. He was dissolving into static, gradually, before my eyes.

I have a lot of homework tonight.

I'll make my famous spaghetti.

He was a hologram. He was a figure made of particles. His eyes looked up at me through a TV screen.

Okay.

He gave me a hug.

Why don't you get dressed up? he said. And put on some of that new perfume.

A girl in a dress looks back at me from the mirror and nods, and lifts the bottle of perfume. She sprays it gingerly on her wrists and behind her ears. She smiles at herself but it is a weak, halfhearted smile, the smile of a girl trying to smile. Her smile is to a real smile what the smell of the perfume is to the smell of real flowers.

My father carried the piping-hot bowl to the table.

Here we go, he said.

The steam rose up, and his head seemed to be floating on a cloud, Wizard of Oz–style.

There were two candles on the table.

Then he brought a bottle of wine. It was already open.

I let it breathe, he said. He poured me half a glass and then filled it up with water.

I don't want you to get drunk on a school night, he said.

After a while I did get a little tipsy, and my head felt heavy and light at the same time. I felt a tingling in my feet, and I took off my shoes. I curled my legs up and crossed them on my chair.

We were talking but I heard our voices from far away. Our words mixed in and out of the music on the CD player and eventually disappeared. We were still talking, I think, but I didn't hear anything. I was just drifting along, not even listening to what I was saying. Then, as if another track of sound were audible for the first time, I could hear what my father was really saying underneath his sentences:

You are getting very sleepy, he said. You are tired and want to lie down.

It was almost funny because his lips were saying something else.

Then I meant to say, I'm not sleepy. But instead I said: The room is spinning.

Are you okay? he said with his mouth. But I heard him, and what he really said was: Go lie down.

You can't make me do this, I thought I said. But what came out was: I can't walk. Will you help me?

He helped me into my room and put me on the bed. I watched him take off my clothes as if I were watching a re-enactment. I saw my leg next to his face. My dress in his hands. Through my hair, I saw his lips say something about midnight.

Then he pulled a nightgown over my head and tucked me in and turned off the light.

That's when I heard the girls' voices. First a whisper, then talking, then laughter. Their voices rose on wings around the room. They seemed to flutter from the walls and up the curtains. Beckett, they said, we miss you.

Beckett, we want to be your friend.

Then the girls appeared in my room, the three dead girls. Their jeans were black with blood. Their hair fell in hardened ropes of blood. They had dark blood under their fingernails.

Why are you here? I asked the girls.

Why are we here? they said, and laughed.

Sunday, the one who had visited me before, was just as mean as the others.

Don't laugh at me, I raised my voice.

Oh, we're scared, they said.

Then they started touching all the things in my room. They picked up the photograph of my mother from the bedside table. They picked up the bottle of perfume from my dresser. They put on lipstick and kissed the poster of Kurt Cobain. Then suddenly, from outside the door, footsteps. That shut them up.

They stood still for a moment in the hazy dark room, like figures behind a scrim.

Then a crack of light came in through the door.

A man and a woman walked into the room. The woman wore sunglasses, and the man was smoking. In the grainy light I couldn't make out their faces, but I could hear the two of them whispering. The woman looked at the girls, tossed her hand, and the girls filed out. Send the others in, she said.

Suddenly the room was filled with candles. And women. Women stood around my bed like surgeons over a patient, only they looked down at me as if they were looking into a fire, their faces flickering and alive. I thought I recognized some of them from the memorial service. One of them looked like Tobey's mother. I looked up at them and asked what was going on, but nothing came out of my mouth. Then they opened their lips, and the sounds of girls' voices rose up, first whispers, then talking, then laughter.

Then, like the sound of an accident, came the severing, mind-dismembering, ragged and unholy sound of a thousand screams.

At the sound of the scream, I was standing in a dark alley, looking at Sunday, Morgan, and Myrrh. This time, a fourth body lay with theirs. It was mine. And a paper label with the words DRINK ME printed on it in beautiful letters was tied around my neck.

part two

1 4

IT WAS A BEAUTIFUL DAY. FROM MY BED I SAW shards of brightness splintered in a water glass, oily rays of pink and yellow swirling in the mirror over the dresser, geometric patterns of sunshine on the floor. Even though everything looked so bright and cheery, I felt a weird sense of dread. The sunlight was too sunny. Later, I realized that I had never really been asleep, or maybe that I would never really wake up again. I was a traveler in a dream, and a dreamer on a dangerous trip. I had been somewhere in the night that I couldn't quite remember, but I had the mysterious feeling that I was still there, in the place beyond dreams, and that I was never going home.

I must have understood more than I let myself know. I must have sensed in my body that something had changed. But even the body can tell a lie. People have psychosomatic illnesses, false pregnancies. They see a white light.

I got out of bed slowly. I sat up, looked at the picture of my mother on the bedside table, and pulled back the covers. In my hand, the comforter was white and the top sheet was white, but underneath me the sheet was red. Underneath me, a rough liquid feeling of wet cotton rubbed against my skin because the sheet was soaked with blood.

At first I thought I was dying. When I figured out what it was, I had to smile. I got out of bed and ran to the bathroom.

In the bathroom, I shoved a handful of toilet paper into my underpants. I looked at myself in the mirror. I looked different. Womanly, I thought.

I stopped in front of my father's door, and stood there. My hand was poised to knock. But I couldn't. I didn't want to talk to him about something like this. I didn't want to watch him handle it.

I picked up the phone and dialed her number.

Pamela?

Who's this?

It's Beckett. I got it.

Got what?

I got it.

There was a long pause.

Oh, she laughed. That's wonderful.

I don't know what to do.

Come see me at school. First thing.

My father's voice came through the door.

I'm coming, I said. I got dressed.

Don't you look happy this morning, he said.

At school I went immediately to the nurse's office. There was a kid with conjunctivitis so I had to wait, but Pamela winked at me when I came in. She gave the kid some ointment and he left.

She closed the door.

Beckett, she said, you're a woman now.

The look in her eyes when she said it was the placid dead look of a mannequin.

Congratulations, she said. She came back to life. She took me in her arms.

Then she took out a box of tampons from a cabinet and told me what to do.

. . .

In class the teacher went on about global warming.

I don't know about everybody else, but I feel pretty hot already.

Thank you, Tobey, the teacher said.

I'm just saying, what's the problem with everything getting hot?

Tobey, would you like to give a presentation about global warming? That would give you an opportunity to look into it further.

Yes, said Tobey, I would like that. A presentation. That sounds good.

It was Pamela who told my dad.

He gave me a hug.

A little while later, when I came out of the bathroom, he was standing outside the door holding a little yellow waste-basket.

I'd like you to use this, he said. In old buildings, the plumbing just can't take it.

It didn't take long for the cramps to come. Sometimes when I was sitting in class, they would sneak up on me like a kicking baby, kneeing me in the abdomen, lightly punching my lower back. They liked to take me by surprise. They seemed to have no sympathy for me. They frightened me and made me sick.

When I got out of class I would go to the bathroom and try to vomit. But nothing came out and I'd just sit there with my pants on and hold my stomach, rocking back and forth.

I tried to get back at the cramps with medicine, but nothing worked. I took all of the over-the-counter options, all the pills with names like undiscovered planets. At night, in bed, victim to the earthquakes in my body, the flowing lava, I tossed and turned and threw the covers around and curled myself into a little ball. My hair fell over the side of the bed, and I kicked off the blanket. My father knocked on the door. He asked if I was okay. He said that maybe we should call a doctor. But I didn't want to worry him so I told him I was all right. I told him it was something I ate.

1 5

THIS IS WHERE IT ALL STARTS TO CHANGE.
This is where the fatal error unfolds and blooms in that deadly,
artificial way of a flower in time-lapse photography. This is
the time when all the mistakes gradually reveal themselves,
petal by petal. Giant flowers shattering on screen, opening
their petals like wings. But the flowers are so beautiful you
don't realize that they're poisonous. You don't realize that if
you get too close they will kill you. Anything that cares only
for beauty can't handle getting close, because from close up,
nothing is only beautiful.

In English class, the teacher talked about a short story. She
said it dealt with the themes of innocence and experience. She
said the words as if they were written in capital letters. She

talked about it as if experience were this dark, awful thing. But what's so bad about experience? Innocence. It sounds like a fucking perfume.

One night I got home late. Pamela was over, and she and my father were sitting at the dinner table, with an empty place set for me.

Where have you been?

With Jen.

Why didn't you call?

I'm sorry. I guess I forgot.

Well, you should have remembered, he said. He was standing up, holding a napkin in his hand. He seemed to have already made the decision to be angry, that he'd decided to play the role of angry dad.

Sit down, he said. Have some dinner.

I just stood there.

He sat back down and started eating. Then he said, I'm just glad you're okay.

I'm okay.

Good.

Guess what, I said.

What. He didn't look up.

I lifted my T-shirt.

I got myself a becoming-a-woman present, I said.

I saw Pamela's eyes go wide.

What? My father lifted his head up and squinted.

A present. I got my belly button pierced. See? It's a tiny silver stud.

I heard the screech of my father's chair as he backed away from the table. He stood up from his chair like a deep-sea monster rising out of the water. I felt his anger move toward me, ahead of him, in a wave.

You have a lot to learn about becoming a woman, he said.

I stood there with my T-shirt lifted a little. I held it tightly in my hand.

What the hell did you do that for? He raised his voice.

I like it. I think it looks cool. I felt a tightness behind my eyes like a metal pipe being twisted.

Well it doesn't look cool.

The pipe burst.

Miles, please.

Why are you so angry? I said.

Miles, please, Pamela said again as my father walked toward me with the napkin in his hand.

Now the tears were down the sides of my face, sliding hot like urine.

Miles, please, she said again. Beckett is trying to share a special moment with you.

Then she turned to me. Beckett, I think your father is a little surprised.

Disgusted, he said. He sounded like he was reading lines.

Miles.

It's okay. Let him say what he thinks.

Miles, you're being very unsupportive.

Because I don't support this kind of thing.

What kind of thing?

Self-mutilation.

I don't believe this.

He stared at me hard: Believe it.

I'm going to my room.

Miles, this is just her way of . . .

I shut the door to my room.

In my room I lay on the bed with music on. Cat curled up next to me, her soft little head floating on the pillow, purring like a battery-operated cat.

Later I went out into the living room, and they were playing Scrabble. It was so cute, I couldn't stand it. I joined in. My father wouldn't speak to me, but at one point he got up to get ice cream and he brought me some.

Is that a word?

Yes, it's a word.

I'm not so sure.

Challenge me. Look it up.

A little while into the game, I doubled over in pain. A knife sliced through me, slashing me, ripping at my insides and cutting through every cord. I dropped the letters in my hand. I heard them fall on the board in gentle clicks like baby teeth.

Are you okay?

I guess it was the ice cream.

Maybe it's your belly button.

Shut up! I yelled.

He was only joking, Pamela said.

I'm sick of his jokes, I said.

Listen, young lady, I'd like to know what's going on.

Nothing's going on, my stomach hurts.

I doubled over in pain.

I tried not to, but I started to cry.

Pamela put her arm around me. Oh, honey, she said. It's okay.

The floodgates opened. I don't know what's going on, I said.

I was up against her breast, and I could smell her perfume. It smelled like what I imagined poppies would smell like. The silk of her shirt went wet with my tears.

You must be so confused, she said.

I felt an infinite rush of gratitude.

So much has happened so quickly, she said. First your mother dies, then a new home, a new school, new friends. Then you meet me, and I meet your father. Now all the changes of becoming a woman.

I could barely listen to what she was saying, but I heard the vibration of her voice through her chest and I felt a blanket of calm fall over me.

Maybe you just need someone to talk to, not me or your dad but somebody else, somebody of your own.

I looked up at her with wet eyes.

I think I know just the person, she said.

At night I stare out the window, watching the living movie of cars and lights. I see the white headlights and red taillights smear across the glossy doors and windshields. I see the green-and-yellow streetlights swim along the hoods of the cars, like neon fish. I see the lights of restaurants and bodegas across the street, floating in the windows, making ghostly rooms inside of rooms.

The reflections soothe me. They make things seem less separate. Everything touching everything.

16

IN THE ROOM, A SUFFOCATING BACKGROUND whoosh like the airless sound inside an airplane.

The woman looked at me steadily. She watched while I blew my nose.

You're very upset about these stomach pains, she said.

I nodded.

You're not sure if they are, as you put it, "real" or psycho-somatic.

I twisted the Kleenex.

You say you take Advil and other medications, even pre-scription medication, and nothing works.

I looked down.

Tell me, Beckett, what else do you think might be causing these cramps?

I don't know.

. . .

You know, it sounds to me, from what you've said, like you've had a pretty rough year. Lots of changes.

She had a diploma on the wall. It was so typical. I stared hard at the gothic lettering. The black lines like wrought iron.

You've been having nightmares.

The wrought-iron gates seemed to open up and let me in.

Yes, I said.

They sound pretty frightening.

Behind the gates, a dark garden.

Terrifying, even.

Yes.

She stood up from her leather chair and walked over to her desk. She opened a drawer and took out a vial. I was watching her through the gates of the garden. Where I was, there were dark roses with dark stems, sinuous vines, webbed canopies of leaves, a black pond. Where she was, there were leather couches and glass tables, pale carpeting, an empty desk.

She sat back down. She leaned forward in her chair. She made eye contact with me as if this were an eye exam.

Beckett, she said, I'm concerned about you.

I looked out the gates. My hair fell between the iron bars, blending in with the twisted pattern.

I think that you're depressed.

She leaned forward a little more.

But you know, Beckett, I don't think you have to be so unhappy.

Oh.

I think you could be a very happy young woman.

You do?

Yes. She paused. She leaned back in her chair. It's not surprising that you feel sad, she said. You've had a painful, complicated year. But I think there's a lot we can do to make it better. I think we should start working together, to really figure out what's going on.

She showed me the vial.

And I'd like you to start taking these.

My hand reached through the gates. She opened the vial and poured two pills into my palm. She handed me a glass of water.

Two of these, three times a day.

I put the pills in my mouth. She smiled a therapeutic smile.

Don't worry, Beckett. We'll get all of this figured out. See you next week.

The gates opened.

1 7

I NEVER WORK IN THE KITCHEN ANYMORE.
It used to be, I would come home from school and sit at the
kitchen table, doing my homework. My father cooking. The
radio on. But now when I get home I go straight to my room.
I lie on my bed. Cat curls up next to me. I listen to music. I listen to myself.

Once, when the pains attacked me, I remember thinking I was
like a magician's assistant, sliced in half. The pains came cutting
through me and I looked down at my feet and they seemed to
be far away, down at the other end of the room. I imagined
them dangling out of the little holes in one of those magician's
boxes, with little sparkling shoes hanging from my toes.

I pulled myself together and stood up. I could barely walk,

and on my way to the door I had to hold on to the dresser. I knocked some nail polish onto the floor. The slicing became a wave of pain, a rolling of anguish through my body, my organs tossed by a sea of blood. But then as quickly as it came, the wave subsided. It rocked evenly. My muscles unroped.

I bent down to pick up the bottle of nail polish from the floor. When I put it back on the dresser, I saw my face in the mirror. For a moment, I didn't recognize myself. I didn't think it was me.

My hair had grown longer, now it rippled below my shoulders, and it was shiny and thick, not thin and stringy. My skin, which had been dull and bumpy, glowed smooth and pale and pink. Even my features seemed changed. My lips looked fuller and redder, the color of watery wine. And my eyes. My eyes had been small and frightened, but now they were wide and clear. They looked out from my face and seemed to reflect back the world. The whites were white, like the white of an egg.

I doubled over in pain. When I looked up again, Pamela's face loomed in the mirror, just behind mine.

Don't cry, she said. You're so young and beautiful.

I didn't know you were here, I said.

For a moment, our faces, like two planets.

Here's your medicine, Beckett. I hope you feel better.

When I took the pills, my hand, in the mirror, touched her face.

1 8

TWO GIRLS ON LINE WITH NICOTINE PATCHES. A boy stuffs crap into one of their backpacks, and the girl doesn't notice. Shit for lunch again, but I'm not hungry. I carry a tray with a Coke and a banana to my table. I hardly eat anymore. All I do is chew gum.

My table is with Jen and a group of girls. The girls talk and talk, and their voices rise like smoke rings. When they laugh, I feel myself inside the laughter, not outside of it, and I let it blow through my hair, a hot wind. I understand the expressions on their faces, the words they use. They mean exactly the opposite of what they say.

He's a genius.

She's cool.

I'm thrilled.

I get up. I clear my tray. I wait on line for the water foun-

tain. When it's my turn, I take out two brightly colored pills.
The girl on line behind me sees the pills.

You too? she says.

She opens her palm. She is holding two brightly colored
pills.

He walked into my room and looked around, and I was em-
barrassed by the posters on the walls and the girlish things on
the dresser and the frills on the edges of the pillowcases. I expected him to look at things carefully, to make fun of me, but
he didn't seem to care about the room.

Hey, Kurt, he said, and gave a little nod.

He sat down on the bed. Then he jumped up and walked
over to the CD player. He looked through my CDs and put one
on. He sat on the bed again. He leaned back. He put his hands
behind his head and stared up at the ceiling, as if he were looking up at the clouds. I noticed the way his shirt tugged around
his shoulders. I saw the line of skin laid bare above his jeans. His
feet were still hanging off the side of the bed. He kicked off his
big sneakers, and they fell to the ground. They lay there, on the
floor, like capsized boats. A shipwreck in my room.

I closed the door and lay down on the bed next to him, my
eyes peeled to the ceiling. His heat poured through me, boil-
ing water over tea leaves. My skin went hot, then cold, then
hot.

I like this song.

So do I.

When his jeans rub up against mine, my legs fill with ginger ale.

What do you think they're saying in this verse?

I have no fucking idea.

We looked at each other. We laughed.

His laugh, his teeth, the slant of his smile. The shadows of his eyelashes like gray strokes of pencil. If only I could read the writing on his face, I thought. The words hidden in the tiny silken lines beneath his eyes. The secret messages spelled in strands of hair.

I know what I want to call my first album, he said.

What?

Grammy-winning Self-titled Debut Album.

I smiled.

His warm hand touched my T-shirt. Dark pink fire shot straight up into my spine.

I rolled over onto my stomach. I looked sideways at him through my hair.

You're so pretty, he said.

I heard the elevator stop in the hallway outside. I heard the

heavy slide of the elevator door. I heard footsteps, keys, the un-
locking, the entry.

Do you want to meet my father? I said.

That night after he goes home, we talk on the phone. I have the
TV on in my room to cover up our conversation. On screen,
the people move like fish in an aquarium. When we stop talking, I look at my reflection in the screen. The people walk
through me. They swim between my eyes. Then I turn off the
image and I see my face in the gray glass. It's eerie. I'm not ugly
anymore.

1 9

ALL OF A SUDDEN I HAD A MILLION FRIENDS.
I went to parties. I went to movies. I had fun.

Sometimes I missed all the time I used to spend alone, so I
took long walks by myself. I felt on these walks that I was
looking for something, something I had lost, but I didn't remember what it was. I looked down the side streets that led to
the river, the streets that appeared to end in nothing, just sky
and a blank space between buildings. I looked at the little
streets downtown, cobblestone streets where I heard voices
from a hundred years ago calling my name, calling me up fire
escapes to where the water towers sat like buddhas, over-
looking the rooftops, meditating. I walked along the river all
the way down to the end of the island, and I watched the birds
winging over the water, the boats rounding the cape of sky-
scrapers, some office buildings like buildings in an old print,

some mirrored new ones that sent the sun shining back to itself in gaudy orange. There were dark churches that seemed to hold ancient sermons in their spires, tall blank buildings where the ghosts of men who had thrown themselves out of windows were still falling, shacks by the water in which sailors from every country, every war, had bought drinks for each other every night. For some reason I was always drawn to the terminal of the Staten Island Ferry, the last outpost of the city, the place where every lonely person ended up. I liked to hang around there and watch the ferries. I liked to feel the wind at the end of the island, and listen to the voices of all the ghosts in the city rising up and blowing across the river.

And there at the end of the world, I would see her. A woman, riding the ferry, staring at me as she pulled away. Dressed in black, standing perfectly still, she looked like a bird, or a bat, flying slowly above the water. She was always facing me, flying backward in some twisted imitation of flight. I could feel her eyes pulling me across the water.

Somewhere inside me I knew who she was, what she wanted, why we were both there. But then I caught a glimpse of my reflection in the dirty window of the ferry terminal, and I remembered that I was beautiful now, that I wasn't sad, and so I decided not to think about the woman on the ferry, who she was, what she meant. It was a decision that occurred so quickly, so deeply, that I never even realized I'd made it.

2 0

IN SCHOOL ONE OF MY NEW FRIENDS SAID to me, Beckett, I like your hair. You have such nice hair.

I do? I said.

You know you do, another one said.

Yeah, Beckett, don't play dumb.

I'm not playing dumb.

One of the girls made a face to another one.

I really hate it when people are falsely modest, she said. It's so phony.

I couldn't believe what was happening. I felt the tension of belonging to the inner circle. I felt sorry for the three dead girls.

I guess I have nice hair, I finally said.

Oh, shut up. Stop bragging, one of them said.

. . .

One night my father and Pamela and I went out to dinner. In the restaurant, men in business suits ate organic goat cheese tortillas and tiny salads drizzled with fancy dressing. Some kids at the next table were listing their favorite resort hotels.

Pamela ordered a glass of red wine. She lifted the glass to her red lips.

The waiter came over. Tonight I have, he said, and he began listing the specials. Pamela looked off at nothing, her long fingers stroking the stem of her wineglass. My father stared at his fork and nodded occasionally, as if he were an anchorman receiving an update through his earphone. I was the only one who looked at the waiter. He wore a crisp white shirt and black pants, and he had chipped polish on his fingernails.

When the food came, my father proposed a toast. He lifted his glass.

I guess you know what I'm going to say, he said.

What? I said.

Well, it's something you've probably suspected for a long time.

I didn't know what he was talking about.

Pamela and I are getting married, he said. He just held his glass there, up in the air.

Wow, I said.

There were tears in his eyes. He looked at Pamela. Her big green eyes were moist too, the surface of a still pond.

Now you'll have a family again, he said to me. He took a sip of wine, as if that had been a toast.

Wow, I said.

Pamela reached over to me and gave me a hug. I'm so honored to be a part of your family, she said. Oh Beckett, she whispered in my ear.

I started to cry.

For some reason, my crying seemed to make my father happy. He smiled, and the tears ran down his cheeks too. Then he collected himself and lifted his glass again.

To family, he said.

To family, said Pamela.

Under the table, I dug my fingers into my leg.

2 1

THE ROOM SPINNING TO MUSIC. HIS HAIR, his jeans, the white moons on his wide fingernails. He touched my face with his hand. He wiped a tear from my neck.

I sat up on the bed. I'm sorry, I said, I don't know why I'm crying.

That's okay, he said.

I just don't understand why he has to marry her. She's over here all the time, anyway.

He was still lying down. I looked down at him, my hair grazing his face.

That tickles, he said.

I shook it all over his face.

He grabbed a hunk of hair and pulled me toward him.

After we kissed for a while, the tears came back.

I don't know what it is, I said.

I reached over to the bedside table and picked up the picture of my mother.

He was leaning back on his arms. You miss her, don't you.

What do you think?

Don't get mad at me.

I fell back down next to him. Sorry, I said.

He touched my face. This time, I wasn't crying.

I heard the elevator moving up and down in the elevator shaft. I heard the cars outside, tuning up like an orchestra. I felt the silver city breeze moving in and out of the window, leaving dust and soot and the faint spray of the river. I could hear the leaves swaying in the park, the meters running in the cabs, the people smoking on the sidewalks.

His tongue moved around in my mouth. His hand played in my hair. He was leaning over me, his heavy boy leg pressing against mine, jeans against jeans.

What time is your father coming home?

I'm not sure. He went for a run, but it could be long.

His mouth was all red from kissing.

But sometimes he takes a short run, I said.

Oh. He rolled onto his back.

You know, Beckett, sometimes when I kiss you I can't tell if you like it.

What do you mean?

You get so quiet and still.

I'm sorry.

You don't have to be sorry. I just want to know if you like it. You don't have to kiss me, you know.

I curled up closer to him. My body went blank and weak, like an empty boat.

But I want to, I whispered.

Why don't you show it?

I thought I did.

You don't.

I didn't say anything for a while. Then I lifted my hand and it felt like someone else's hand, detached from me, as if I were holding a hand, not using it. I reached up to his face and stroked his hair back. Then I pulled myself up and leaned over him. My hair snaked over his face like seaweed. This time he didn't say it tickled.

When I kissed him he slipped loose from the bottom of the ocean and we drifted out on a wave.

We spend all our time together now. When he jokes in class, his jokes are for me. When he smiles, I see it all the way across the cafeteria.

After school he comes to my house or I go to his or we talk on the phone. I don't think of him as a separate person but as a face, a shoulder, a hand. His words run through my head at night as I fall asleep. I hear the way he says my name, and that becomes my name. I see his hair in my dreams falling over his face, his smile like the tilted angle of a hat. He dances with me in dreams, an old soft shoe, he spins me into room after room. Sometimes when I see his long awkward legs or his funny handwriting, I think it can't be him, not the person who swoops me down into a dip in my sleep, who sings me awake, but then he cracks me up with some silly handshake or I see the hidden, hurting messages in his wondering look and I can't remember ever being anywhere except with him, anyplace except now, not ever.

Beckett, he says, you're like ketchup.

What's that mean?

You make everything better.

From his smile it's hard to tell if he means it, but I know he does. He doesn't lie to me.

That day we were on my bed doing homework. Tobey started playing with my hair. Then he touched my face. I felt a water-fall down my spine. We started kissing. I felt a river in my legs.

At the bottom of the river it was dark and cool. We swam around for a while, the bubbles spilling upward, as we talked to each other underwater. I could see rays of sunlight slicing through the water, the white froth of the waterfall crashing in the distance, little pink-and-blue fish.

Underwater, Tobey swam up to me. He pressed his body into mine. Silver bubbles exploded when our bodies touched, and the hundreds of pink-and-blue fish scattered. They swam off like synchronized swimmers in an old movie. The rays of sunlight underwater turned rainbow colors, orange and purples split into prisms, a thousand diamonds sparkling overhead.

We lingered in this trippy, underwater paradise like a couple of dolphins at Sea World. I think, Am I crazy? Am I sane? What's real? What's fake? But the questions rise in bubbles from my head and drift away. I don't want to know the answers.

When I opened my eyes, Tobey was on top of me and I couldn't move. He was lifting my shirt ever so slightly, and touching the cool skin on my stomach. Then his hand moved up, under my shirt. After a while his hand moved down and he unzipped my jeans. I heard something outside in the hall and turned my head. That's when I saw her. She was standing in the doorway. Her eyes were emeralds, sharp and clear. She was staring at us. She was staring at us and the look on her face was dead like the look of the sky before it erupts into lightning.

I stare back at her, my eyes locked into the green. I will not look away. Tobey's hand slips under my jeans. I feel a shudder. Then my eyes roll back in my head and all I can see is bright white, the white of a million stars.

2 2

TOBEY LEFT BEFORE DINNER. IT WAS JUST me and my father and Pamela. They were talking about their wedding, but I wasn't really even listening. I was thinking about Tobey. About halfway through the meal, I realized that Pamela was looking at me differently. She seemed far away, like she was playing the part of Pamela but she wasn't really there. Her face was Pamela's, and her hands were Pamela's, but she moved like a movie that was shot to be shown in slow motion and then sped up to normal speed, and you could tell there was something wrong, unreal. She was angry. I could feel it.

She stood up to clear the table. She smiled when she did it. She held her hand out for my plate. She smiled. The frame froze.

. . .

This happens to me: The frame freezes, and I see what's really going on.

It's strange, but I need to see things as a movie in order to see the truth. Most of the time, I believe in what's going on. But when the frame freezes, I see that everyone has been acting. Most of the time, I'm so gullible. But when I have these moments, when the frame freezes, I see that I'm surrounded by fucking movie stars.

She decided to make dessert. It was some kind of fruit and ice cream and liqueur concoction. She never cooked. It tasted delicious, but she just watched us eat.

Maybe we should serve this at the wedding, my father said.

Maybe, she said. She moved her head quickly, like a bit of a maniac. Do you like it, Beckett?

Yeah, it's pretty good.

Do you think Tobey would like it?

I don't know.

You don't know?

How would I know?

You're pretty close with him, aren't you?

Yeah, but I can't read his mind.

Oh, but when you love somebody, you can read their mind.

Can anyone read my mind? my father said. I want to watch the news.

Secrets pass between us, shadows hiding in shadows. In the movie in my mind, a man creeps up the stairs. A bird lands. A woman passes a cup of tea, and suddenly we know it's poisoned. A girl runs. A knife slashes. She knows that he knows that she knows.

I threw myself on the bed.

I'm so glad it's you, I said.

It's me, he said.

I closed my eyes. I feel like I'm in prison.

I know, he said. I miss you so much.

We hung on the phone awhile, just breathing.

Then he said, I feel like something special is happening between us.

Uh-huh.

Do you know what I'm talking about.

Our breath moved like wind back and forth across the phone line, and it sounded like breathing underwater.

Yes.

I was lying on my back with a pillow on my stomach. The shadows of headlights drove across the ceiling.

I feel ready, he said.

I rolled over on my side and whispered, Me too.

I shut my eyes tight. I wish you could be here, I said.

I can.

How?

If you leave the key in the hall, I can get into your apartment.

What about the doorman?

Just tell him to let me in. Go downstairs before you go to bed and tell him.

Really?

Really, he said. I mean, if you want me to come.

I want you to.

I'll be there at midnight.

The sound of his breath like the sound of the wind.

I love you, Beckett.

I love you too.

I'll see you tonight.

Good-bye.

Good-bye.

Hello? Hello? Who's there?

Click.

Hello?

. . .

I told my father that I left a book in the lobby and that I needed to go get it. I went downstairs and spoke to the doorman. He was a young guy who was always reading. These days, with my long hair and my new smile, he would look at me when I left the building, and look up when I came in. I told him I wanted to tell him a secret. I told him I had a friend coming. I really had changed. He gave me the most sickening smile.

I waited up for Tobey with the TV on and the sound off. Pamela and my father went to sleep early, and I took the kitchen TV into my room.

At midnight, nothing happened. I waited in my room, listening for the elevator, but it wasn't moving. Around twelve-fifteen it shook and sighed and lifted off, but it went right past our floor. At about twelve-twenty I stood up and stared out the window, but I didn't have a view of the front of the building and I didn't know which way he would come.

I saw a few trees shiver a little and some cars go by, but no people. The emptiness frightened me. It occurred to me that maybe the doorman had faked me out—I saw his sickening smile—that he had no intention of letting Tobey up. But then I thought that Tobey would probably call, even risk waking up my father, just to let me know he was okay. He always called.

I kept the TV on. Late at night, television becomes unbearably sad, all the loneliness, the miles of empty space, the hosting of guests, the endorsing of products, all happening in this deep-space black hole of nighttime like a long, boring dream that keeps you half awake. One minute I was flipping the channels like crazy. It was all one long show. But then the next minute I would be really into something, a recipe or a testimonial or a subplot.

The whole time, I could see my face in the screen, electric images running through my visible brain, and after a while I had the scary feeling that what was playing on television was actually what was happening in my mind.

23

THE LIGHT IN THE COFFEE SHOP IS PISS yellow. It pools in the lid of the little metal milk pitcher, making weird, smeary reflections of the boys at the table. Knives and forks dance around in the air when the boys talk. Food lands on the table because they spit when they get excited, and when they laugh they don't care about closing their mouths. They tell story after story until it becomes one long story, and they pedal backward and refer to something someone said ten minutes earlier and that becomes the joke of the night as they repeat it endlessly, making it funnier each time, more coded and more meaningless. They jostle each other under the table, their long legs interwoven with one another's like the teeth of a comb, their knees touching the underside of the table, where hard gum and old spills tell stories of other nights, other boys.

. . .

Toad, watch my food, man. Keep your mouth shut when you chew.

Oh, Mr. Clean. Excuse me. I didn't think you cared what you ate.

That's right, he eats whatever he can. He's a donkey boy.

You too, Crater.

Get that the fuck off my plate.

Now you're making me laugh, man.

Toad, you eat it. You like to eat.

No, he has to save his appetite for the real thing.

Tobey throws a fry from the floor onto the guy's plate.

I'm just speaking the truth.

You're my Zen master.

Really, what's it like getting so much?

Shut the fuck up.

Cut it out with the dirty fries, man. That's been on the floor.

He likes it when they make him eat it from the floor.

Down, slave! Lick it up off the floor.

Question: Which is more dangerous, being a dominatrix or, like, a race car driver?

What the fuck?

I mean, which is the more dangerous profession?

Quit with the fries, I'm not kidding.

I mean, think about it, these women, they, like, meet up with anybody, these crazy CEO types or these serial killers, who knows, and they do this shit.

What the fuck are you talking about?

I know what he's talking about. I read this article.

Yeah, you know because your father likes it that way.

Hey, your mother.

Watch it with the spitting, okay. I'm gonna have to make a fucking barricade around my fucking hamburger.

Hey, can I get another Coke? Thank you.

Well, Toad would know about this. He's Mr. Experienced.

Fuck you, Crater.

You're so testy tonight.

Let's get the check.

What, it's not even midnight.

Look. Wait, don't look right away. Not all you idiots at once. See that babe?

What babe?

Leather boots.

Yeah.

You think that's a wig?

Definitely.

No, Hirsch's mom has hair like that.

Shut up.

That looks like one of Crater's dominators. Or whatever the fuck they're called.

I think she's been looking at us.

Oh, you flatter yourself, Zen master.

How the fuck can you tell? She's got sunglasses on.

I wonder if she has a black eye.

Oh that's good, Crater. Very nice. You're a scary son of a bitch.

Let's ask her Hirsch's question, about the dangerous profession. Excuse me, ma'am . . .

Put your fucking hand down.

I gotta go.

What?

I gotta go.

Tobey throws a ten-dollar bill on the table.

Where you gotta go?

No fucking way. Don't go yet. We haven't even started.

Started what? Pissing the night away?

What the fuck is the matter with you?

I'm late for an appointment.

Who with?

Who do you think? His girlfriend.

Yo, girlfriend . . .

Yeah, you wish you had a girlfriend.

Hirsch is his girlfriend.

Really, you're meeting Beckett?

I'm going to her house.

What's the deal with her, anyway? She's so quiet.

She's a race car driver.

She's a Zen master.

You fucking keep your big mouth shut when you laugh, man, and keep your fucking already-chewed food off my plate, you . . .

She's smart, that's all.

Ooh, smart.

Listen, I gotta go.

But we love you, Tobey.

Yeah, we'll let you lick it up off the floor.

Thanks, thanks a lot you assholes. Have a pleasant evening.

The Toad's gotta go . . .

He's got to go . . .

Tobey makes his way to the back of the restaurant. He tries the pay phone but it's broken.

Excuse me, is this your only phone?

There's another downstairs.

Thanks.

He walks down a dirty flight of stairs, food stains on the walls and a sticky coating of grime on the steps, a sickly sweet smell of disinfectant, a smell of roses smothered in butter-scotch laced with insecticide. Downstairs, it's a cramped space, three black doors, a pay phone, and a dismal-looking corridor that opens onto a shaft full of garbage. Someone's on the phone, a tall guy with a sleazy beard, so Tobey goes to the bathroom. He sees three doors, each marked by a gold rec-tangular sticker with black writing: *Men, Women,* and *Private.* Private must be that third sex, he thinks. He pushes open the door to the men's room. As he slips in, he sees the sexy babe from the counter slip into the women's room. He has a brief fantasy about her, something involving legs pressed up against a sink.

Inside, it stinks: urine, semen, cigarettes, shit, mustard, vomit, misery. There's a toilet opposite the door, and a tiny, filthy sink. He unzips his fly but nothing comes out. He's still thinking about the babe next door. Standing there with his fly open, he can hear the sleazy guy on the phone. His voice is murmuring, nervous. When the guy hangs up, Tobey finally starts to pee. He tries to hurry it up because he doesn't want anyone else to get to the phone. He pictures Beckett's eyes, he sees them watching him, and just at that moment the door opens behind him. It opens behind him with a push so strong that he falls forward a little in the tiny room. What the fuck? he says. Excuse me, someone's in here. He doesn't turn around right away because his fly is open, and he says, I'll be out in a second. Then he says, What the fuck?

As he zips up his fly, he turns around, and then he sees her, the babe from upstairs. She has sunglasses on, and she's wearing lipstick and a leather coat and leather boots. She looks like some kind of parody of glamour. She has a furious aura, the halo of a devil, a purple haze emanating from her as if she exists inside the light of a black lightbulb. For a second he thinks he's imagining all this, that it's some crazy extension of his fantasy. He half expects her to lean up against the sink and spread her legs, but she doesn't do that at all.

What she does is make a hissing sound. It seems to come from the back of her throat, and in the ghastliness of the moment he thinks he sees into her mouth. She has the tongue of a snake. The tongue is dark pink, and it flutters like mad when she lets out a hiss. He shrinks in the corner and opens his mouth, but nothing comes out. She reaches into her pocket. Her hand comes out of her pocket, and her arm rises over her head. She has a bottle of ketchup in her hand. Tobey looks up and sees the bottle and pleads with his eyes, but still nothing comes out of his mouth. Then the bottle swings down on his head.

As the instrument hits his head, he slumps against the wall. It is a vicious, mythic violence. She comes down on him with the bottle like some raging angel, hacking her way through heaven with a machete. Her fury spreads like wings, and the room seems to grow in order to contain her, coloring as the bottle breaks, bleeding around her in an explosion of red. She swings and slashes in an inconsolable madness until she descends into the desolate center of the storm, the room around her a bloodshot eye. For a moment, a sudden peace. The boy on the floor. The shards of glass in the sink. The sound of the restaurant continuing up above. Then footsteps on the stairs, and she is gone though the open door into an alleyway, into the dead of night.

2 4

WHEN I WOKE UP IT WAS AFTER THREE. I
felt an immediate wave of rejection, then longing, and then despair. My first thought was: I want to kill myself. Actually, it
was a little different. It was a voice in my head, the voice of
Sunday, the beautiful girl, and it was saying, *You should kill yourself.* I felt a heaviness inside. It was a feeling I remembered
from when my mother died.

I got out of bed and looked pointlessly out the window. The
trees had stopped shivering. The city was very, very still. Then
I saw my reflection take shape in the window and I froze with
a mixture of terror, shame, and pride.

I fell back to sleep, certain that Tobey had changed his mind
and decided not to come. He'd realized that he didn't love
me. I cried myself back to sleep. Right as I was drifting off, I
thought I heard the elevator stop on our floor. But I knew it

wouldn't be him. Cat came in and curled up on me. I got so upset that I started to think my whole time with Tobey had been a joke, a cruel trick, or worse, that I'd made it up and it had never happened.

In the morning, when the alarm rang, he wasn't there.

2 5

I LEFT FOR SCHOOL WITH A PIT IN MY
stomach, and as soon as I got there I knew that something was
wrong. I didn't see Tobey anywhere. He wasn't in the cafeteria, and he wasn't hanging out with the band in the auditorium. I went to history, and his seat was empty. Then I cut
English to go to the diner with Jen while she had a cigarette,
and I told her what happened.

Why didn't you call him?

I don't know.

You're so insecure, she said.

Two guys walked in.

Hey.

Hey.

Hey.

Hey.

They stood by our booth like waiters.

Have fun with Tobey last night?

Shut the fuck up, Jen said.

They laughed and sat at their own booth.

Later in the day I asked one of them what he meant. He'd wiped off the smirk from the diner and had plastered on a little-boy obedient look, his teacher face. He tried to keep his eyes from staring at me, and so they wandered all over, at the lockers, at other kids. He had light brown facial hair, almost pink.

He told me that Tobey had been with him and the other guys last night and that he'd been planning to come to my house. He said he'd left the coffee shop before the rest of them. He didn't know what time. I could tell by the way my heart dropped into my legs like an elevator with no cables that he was telling the truth.

Tobey's mother picks up the phone. Her voice low and throaty, it sounds like it's hiding its face from the cameras. I ask for Tobey and she tells me he is in the hospital. She says he's in a coma. She says she has to go.

They looked at me with expressions of helplessness and worry. His arm rested unsteadily around my shoulder. She held a glass of water in one hand, and in the other, two brightly colored pills.

I took the pills and the water, but it wasn't me. It was my body, but it wasn't me.

At first, I couldn't find out anything. Eventually they told me that Tobey had been attacked that night in the coffee shop, in the men's room. That's all they'd say. He was in critical condition and they wouldn't let me visit him. Doctor's orders, they said.

2 6

I SAT ON THE COUCH. I LOOKED AT THE wall. I saw the black lettering. I walked through the gates.

I could hear the blank purr of the white-noise machine, but from beyond the gates, it sounded like rain.

She handed me another Kleenex.

You feel that your conversation with Tobey had something to do with his illness, she said.

Coma, I said.

Coma. Yes.

You feel that you caused Tobey to go into a coma. You feel responsible, she said.

I looked at her from beyond the gates. Vines covered her face. I felt the rain.

What did you talk about in your phone conversation?

I don't know. We talked. It was nice.

Did you talk about anything in particular?

I already told you. He was going to come over. That's when I heard the click.

Yes. The "click." Tell me about that.

After he hung up, I heard a click. Like someone else was on the line, hanging up.

Were you upset that he hung up?

No. We'd said good-bye.

Did saying good-bye upset you?

The rain snaked down the back of my neck.

What happened before you said good-bye?

Nothing, I said.

The rain poured down my face.

Beckett, would you like another Kleenex? Why don't I give you the box?

Okay.

You were going to tell me what happened right before he said good-bye, and then you began to cry.

I was trying to reach her, but the vines were thick. Then I said, Right before he said good-bye, he told me that he loved me.

I started to cry again.

And that meant a lot to you, she said.

Lightning struck a tree. It lit up the garden. I saw roses floating on a black pond.

It seems like it meant a lot to you, Beckett, to hear that you were loved.

Lightning struck again and it lit up the trees. Their thin arms pleading with heaven, dripping with rain.

Beckett, I think it's going to take a while to get to the bottom of all of this. In the meantime . . .

She stood up. She walked quietly across the carpet to her desk. She came back.

I'd like to readjust your medication. I'd like you to try these.

She handed me two green pills. I took them. Then she handed me the bottle.

Let's keep a very close watch on things. Call me if you need to talk.

The garden fell dark. I walked along matted leaves in my bare feet. I reached for the gates. I pushed them open.

Then she leaned forward in her chair and looked at me as if she were reading my brain through my eyes.

Remember, Beckett, she said, you have a very active imagination. I think your conversation with Tobey stirred up a lot of feelings inside you, and sometimes your feelings feel overwhelming. But I don't think you need to worry. We'll figure it all out.

The iron gate was heavy and cold and wet. I let it slip out of my hand, behind me.

2 7

THEY WERE MARRIED IN THE LIVING ROOM.

There were about sixty people. Pamela filled the place with white votive candles in little glasses, the size of shot glasses, each one a swig of light. She got lots of flowers, white mostly, but her bouquet was red roses. A judge performed the ceremony. She wore a black robe.

My father was wearing a new suit, and Pamela had on a short white wool dress with no sleeves. She held on to her bouquet really tightly, and the roses pressed up against her dress.

I was standing right near her, just off to the side. I guess I was a bridesmaid or a flower person. My hair had gotten really long, and I had a garland of tiny roses for my head, and a long velvet dress. I tried to look really solemn. I focused all my attention on Pamela's bouquet so that I wouldn't listen to what the judge was saying and start to cry.

. . .

I listened closely to the sounds from the street below, a honk, a cry, the slide of wheels. I was out there on the street, walking with my mother. The city night wrapped us in a blue wind. The sky stretched lavender and pink behind a black silhouette of buildings. The lights went off in the stores, and on in the windows. People looked for each other on every street, everyone searching for something, for themselves. I held my mother's hand and I squeezed it tightly. She squeezed mine back. We turned a corner into the night.

When the ceremony was finished, everybody clapped, like at a play. People came over to me and gave me kisses. They kept telling me how pretty I looked. I picked up Cat and sat on the couch with her in my lap, talking to a magazine-editor friend of my dad's. He was probably almost forty. He was hitting on me. He kept tilting his head and looking at me with this kind of coy expression that made me sick. I just looked down at Cat and ruffled her fur.

Do you like school? he asked.

Do you like your job? I answered.

He laughed.

I remember the last time I saw you, he said. You seemed much younger.

I probably was, I said.

No, it was just a few months ago. Don't you remember?

Maybe. I don't know.

Man, you're tough.

What do you mean?

I mean, you don't even try to be charming, do you?

Cat rolled over in my lap, and I scratched her stomach.

Why should I? I said.

You were such a sweet kid last time I saw you.

Maybe you're thinking of someone else.

I'm not. But you were different.

Sorry.

Don't be sorry. You've gotten sexy.

A hot chill rushed across my skin. Cat jumped out of my lap and walked away.

He tilted his head a little more. You've gotten complicated, he said. He took a sip of champagne and kept his eyes on me.

I think women are much more complicated than men, he said.

A rose petal fell out of the garland on my head. It looked like a drop of blood against my dress.

What do you think? he said.

I wanted to look up and speak to him in tongues. I wanted to vomit equations on his face.

He tried to make eye contact. I looked away. A jazz trio was playing in a corner of the room, and a couple of people in white shirts were serving hors d'oeuvres and champagne from trays. He kept tilting his head in that obnoxious way to follow my gaze and get my attention. Finally, he gave up. He looked down at his glass of champagne and then lifted it to his lips. I finally looked at him. He took a sip of champagne.

Women are more complicated, he said, but men are more interesting.

A woman sat down next to him, and he shifted his position. I got up and spoke to a friend of Pamela's. She was the mother of a girl who was in the class below me. The mother had dark hair and bangs, and she was wearing a suit. She told me that Sara, her daughter, really looked up to me.

Sara says that she and her friends took a vote and that you're the older girl they'd most like to be.

That's flattering, I said.

It is, she said. She smiled a social smile. She had a little smear of lipstick on her teeth.

I hear you have a very cute boyfriend, she said.

Who the fuck is your daughter? I thought. Some kind of spy?

He is cute, but actually, he's sick right now. He's in the hospital, I said.

Oh dear. What's the matter?

He's in a coma.

As a waiter came by I took a glass of champagne from his tray. I took a long sip.

That's awful, she said. She appeared concerned.

We looked into each other's eyes for a moment. I noticed

that her eyes looked much older than the rest of her face. Not the skin around her eyes, but the eyes themselves. It was like she was looking out from behind one of those gorilla masks, only her face was smooth and almost attractive. But her eyes darted around through a couple of holes, and they were shadowy, like the eyes in an old movie.

Then she lowered her voice and squinted at me.

Tell me, she said, was it drugs?

I tried to see the space between her mask and her eyes, but I couldn't.

Yeah, I said. Lots of drugs.

I finished off the champagne and put it back on another tray.

I saw Pamela across the room, talking to some women from her book group. The women seemed to dote on Pamela. They touched her dress and fixed her hair. They reminded me of characters in a religious painting, like they were posing for a picture at the same time as they were witnessing some profound, spiritual event. They wore what my history teacher would have called the traditional garments of the period, and they had an ancient, ageless look in their eyes.

I walk down the hall to the bathroom. It's a long, dark hall with closets along the sides, and I feel the narrowness of it close around me. The bathroom door is shut. I knock on it before turning the old glass doorknob, but no one answers. I open the door and turn on the light. The light comes on in a flash of yellow, and in that flash I see a shape move on the toilet seat.

It is Cat. She is perched on the toilet seat and drinking from the bowl. I shoo her off and say Cat, get down from there, but she won't move. I reach down to pick her up, and when I look into the bowl, I see that it is filled with blood.

The blood sits in the bowl like a sacred symbol, a message, a warning, a sign. It seems deeper than red, almost blue, almost gold, almost black. In the moment of fear, I see it spill out of the bowl and fill the room; I feel it splash, hot and thick, across my face. Then the fear dies down and I see that the blood is just a liquid, nothing but a surprise. But as the loud, throaty sound of the flush fills my head and I turn off the light, I know the blood means something. I know that the blood is not just a surprise. I know that it is meant for me.

2 8

I SPENT MORE TIME AT JEN'S HOUSE. JEN had a group of friends, an alliance of girls who were pretty and cool. Jen was the smartest. I remember when I'd first met her, she'd seemed like a loner, but now here she was, the center of attention.

Jen's parents were divorced and her mother was usually in bed watching TV. One time I went to get something to drink from the refrigerator and I reached for a pitcher of orange juice. Not that, that's my mom's juice, Jen said. It was thin and watery. Her mother was a drunk, and Jen never said anything about it.

. . .

I called the hospital every day. Sometimes I got through to Tobey's mother, but she usually sounded too distraught to talk to me, and some relative would take the phone away from her and say she couldn't speak now. I tried to visit but they wouldn't let me in. I got as far as Tobey's room. It was at the end of a long corridor lined with wheelchairs and nurses and visitors and patients. I saw the faces of the people as I walked along the hall, and I realized that it was impossible to tell who was healthy and who was sick.

The five of us were sitting around Jen's room, smoking.

You like this color on me? Maya asked.

No, Jen said.

Thanks, Maya said.

Fuck that color. That color is ugly.

How about this?

Maybe you should wear just like a garter belt and a trench coat, Sofia said.

Who's this guy, anyway? I asked.

He's a rock star.

No, he isn't.

He looks like one.

He does, kind of. But he's nice, Maya said.

Nice, Jen said. That's such a bad word.

Yeah, Chloe said. What the hell does nice mean?

Jen put out her cigarette and rolled off the bed. She walked to the bookshelf. She took out the dictionary.

Here, she said. She threw the dictionary to Sofia.

That's so fucking heavy, Sofia said.

Let me look it up, Chloe said. Oh, fuck, my nails aren't dry. You look it up. She handed the book to me.

Maya was still trying on clothes in front of the mirror. The closet doors were open, and there were clothes all over the floor. Sofia was lying on the rug, her long legs stretched out in front of her, her body bent like a hinge, painting her toenails black. Chloe walked over to the dresser to put a new topcoat on her fingers. There was a mirror over the dresser, and from the chair where I was sitting I could see an abstract reflection in the mirror, a painting of hair and skin and sweaters and jeans. A song about love was playing on the CD player. It made me think of Tobey.

Nice, I said. I pushed my hair over my shoulder and cleared my throat. Nice. A small port in the South of France.

Beckett's so funny. Isn't Beckett funny?

Beckett should do stand-up.

Beckett is genius.

Shit, I said. I doubled over and looked under my chair.

What is it?

She's just joking.

No, she isn't.

Beckett, what's the matter? Jen came over to me. Can I get you something?

I've got bad cramps, I said.

Shit, Chloe said. I heard her blow on her nails.

I'll get you something, Jen said.

Bring out the drugs, Sofia said.

Maya walked over from the mirror and handed me her cigarette.

A few puffs always make my cramps go away.

I took a few puffs. The smoke filled my lungs with a gray heat. It helped. But then the lava came back.

I doubled over again.

Try stretching in this position, Sofia said. She went into some contorted yoga move. My mother's trainer taught me this.

Take these, Jen said.

I've already taken ten of those today.

Beckett, you should really go to the doctor.

Yeah, you always have cramps.

I took the pills.

I'm okay, I said. I told Pamela about it, and she's a nurse, and she said it's normal.

Yeah, but she's only a school nurse.

Jason told me he had sex with her.

Everybody says they had sex with her.

Shut up. She's married to Beckett's dad.

Get out, Chloe said.

It's true, Jen said. Anyway, Jason's full of shit.

Beckett, you should see a real doctor.

The fire twisted inside me like flaming vines. There was a garden inside me, and it was slowly burning. The naked arms of the trees were on fire. The gates were on fire. The roses that floated on the pond were on fire, flames scattered across the water.

Beckett, are you okay?

I had fainted and they were looking down at me. Their long hair falling down, silky rain.

29

WHEN I GOT HOME I WENT STRAIGHT TO
the bathroom. The corridor, the doorknob, the light. I sat
down on the side of the tub, my insides crashing like waves
against rocks. I fumbled under the sink for a box of tampons.
I saw my reflection in the metal base of the old sink, my
twisted face, my convex skull. I looked like I was trapped inside the base of the sink, pressing my pretty face against the
barrier between me and the world.

For an instant I saw myself trapped in Dr. Kent's book.
She'd told me she was writing a book with some title like "The
Death of the American Teenager." I looked at myself and
thought, I'm a case study.

*Current events, if it's possible to use such a quaint term anymore
in our global-media-information age, reveal to us that the American
teenager is in serious trouble, if not on the verge of extinction. It is my*

belief that in one girl's story——I'll call her Beckett——there is a clue, a way inside the problem . . .

The box toppled over, and the tampons spilled all over the black-and-white-tiled floor. It looked like a skeleton has collapsed. I started to collect them and stuff them back in the box. I was crawling on the cold tiles. Down on the floor, I was eye level with the little yellow wastebasket my father gave me. I looked inside. I had gone to the bathroom earlier in the day and used a tampon. I had thrown it away. But now the wastebasket was empty.

I stood up and looked at my face in the mirror over the sink. I didn't look trapped and distorted anymore. I looked radiant. My eyes looked into my eyes. They were clear and understanding. I smiled, and I smiled back. I opened the medicine cabinet and took out my pills. I aligned the arrows. I pushed off the childproof cap. Then I opened the bottle of pills and I poured them into the sink and watched as they marched like a million insects. I watched as they spiraled down the drain.

30

THE RED LINE ZOOMS AROUND IN A CIRCLE like a demented conductor's baton. I watch the clock above the blackboard. The seconds go so quickly, but the minutes take forever.

I put my head down on the desk. I felt the hard waxy surface against my arms and face and I tried to console myself with the simple pain of it. My cramps were so bad and the sirens in my brain so loud that I gave up distracting myself and prepared to die. That was when I saw Tobey, sitting in his usual seat, eating a plate of fries at his desk. I had gotten used to staring at his empty seat. Then one day I realized I'd forgotten exactly what he looked like, the exact expression of his face. He'd been gone only a few weeks, but it felt like I'd known him only in some parallel world.

Now, as soon as I closed my eyes, he appeared to me, first banging on the back of a ketchup bottle, then dipping his fries into the ketchup, then eating a fry and handing me another.

At first it was obviously a dream. Tobey would appear to me when I closed my eyes, sitting at his desk, eating the fries. He turned and smiled at me, and I smiled back. He mouthed some words, and I tried to decipher them, but then suddenly I heard a loud click and I opened my eyes.

Two minutes had gone by. I sat up in my seat and watched the teacher's head bobbing in front of a background of numbers. I gave up on Tobey. But then a few minutes later the sound of laughter seemed to rise up from outside the classroom, and I leaned a little in my chair to look. That was when I saw him standing in the hall, dressed in his favorite jeans and his Suck T-shirt, his hair falling into his eyes.

He stands there, peering into the classroom through the window in the door, and after a little while I get up and leave the room.

Hey, I said.

Hey, he said.

He seemed shy. He kicked the wall a couple of times, gently.

Listen, he said, I really miss you.

I miss you too.

Two kids ran down the hall, right past us.

What happened that night? I said. Why didn't you come?

Somebody tried to kill me, he said.

Who tried to kill you?

Come on, Beckett, you know who.

His eyes looked right through me.

It seemed crazy that we were having this conversation, but I felt the heat of him next to me. I felt his breath.

He didn't say anything more. He took a lighter out of his pocket and started flicking it on and off. Then he flicked it on and kept it on. The flame rose in the air, red, white, and blue. He held the lighter with one hand and put the other above the flame. He lowered his hand into the flame. Then he motioned for me to do the same thing. He took my fingers. We held hands inside the flame. I held on tightly and I felt the heat, the scorch of it, the red of it, the white, the blue. For a long time we held hands in the burning heat, without pain, without being afraid.

The fire spread through my body. I told Tobey it was getting too hot, and I asked him to turn off the lighter. But he wasn't there. I was sitting outside the classroom on the floor of the hall, my spine against the wall, my legs bent, and my hands clutching my knees. The heat of the flame became the familiar ache in my body. My cramps were back.

3 1

THE SMOKE FILLS MY LUNGS WITH EXHAUST, with heat. I feel the tissues in my body light like embers. They glow and fade to gray. Jen takes the joint from my hand, and I see her pass it to Chloe, like deep-sea divers pointing things out to each other underwater.

You saw him in the hallway?

That's what she said, Jen said.

Ten minutes must have gone by. The music spun around.

You know where I want to go? said Chloe.

Where? said Jen.

Venus, said Chloe.

I can't wait.

Jen took a long drag. She started to roll another.

Do you think the other planets will turn out to be like ours? Chloe asked.

I'm sure, Jen said.

They both cracked up.

They probably all have shitty guys and bad movies, Chloe said.

Coming soon to a Venus theater near you, Jen said, a witty and scathing satire of our media-saturated society.

That's good, Chloe said.

You could tell she was trying to think up something funny to say back, but couldn't.

I gotta go, I said.

Don't go, Chloe said. You haven't helped me figure out what to wear.

That'll make her stay, Jen said.

You haven't told us all about your visit from Tobey, Chloe said. She rolled over from her back to her stomach, and her hair fell in her face.

There's not that much to tell.

Do you think it was a ghost? Like Hamlet's father?

I think she was smoking this stuff in class.

No, Jen, I believe her.

That made me feel weird. The only person who believed me was Chloe. And she was an idiot.

. . .

When I got home from school, the apartment was empty. Pamela was at class, and my father was out, having a drink with some editor. I walked in the door and threw my knapsack on the floor. I kicked off my shoes—Pamela had a Zen thing about no shoes on in the apartment—and went to the kitchen. Someone had left the little television on.

Coming up on the hour . . . Tonight at nine . . . The TV sounded like some loser trying to get attention.

There was nothing in the cabinet. Only things that needed to be cooked. Cat strolled into the kitchen and rubbed up against my jeans.

What should I eat? I asked her.

She rubbed hair all over the bottom of my pants.

It was an old refrigerator, nothing fancy like an ice machine. No self-defrosting mechanism or water dispenser. The freezer sat on top, and it usually overflowed with frost. Inside, it kept the ice cream burnt. I looked around the main cabin. Suddenly a drip fell onto the metal rim of the shelf. I assumed that the freezer couldn't take it anymore and was bulging open with frost that had begun to melt. Then another drop fell. The second drop landed on the white plastic floor of the refrigerator. It was bright red, and it splattered into a little flower.

I stood up and got a paper towel. Instinctively, I cleaned up the spill. While my hand was in the refrigerator, another drop fell, this time onto the plastic wrap around a dish of leftovers. I wiped that drop. Then I stood up and closed the refrigerator door. I threw the paper towel in the garbage can. I went back to the refrigerator and opened it again.

Inside, the freezer is stuffed. In the front I see all kinds of frozen foods. I push them aside. Way in the back there seem to be things wrapped up in layers of tin foil. In the back of the freezer, frost lines the walls. The frost is dark red.

When I opened my eyes, I was lying on my bed, and Pamela was leaning over me. As soon as I woke up, she started questioning me. She spoke in a whisper. She was calm because she was not the one who had fainted.

How do you feel? she said.

Okay, I said.

You fainted like a lady in a Victorian novel, she said.

Her hair hung down above me and nearly touched my face. She pushed it behind her ear.

I saw you just as I walked into the room, she said. You collapsed. You swooned. It was terrifying.

I didn't hear you come in, I said.

What were you doing?

Looking for something to eat.

Did you have lunch?

Not really. My cramps are bad.

Your blood sugar must have been low. Did you feel dizzy?

That jump-cut, maniac look in her eyes.

What were you looking for in the refrigerator?

I tried to roll slightly to the left, but her hands were on either side of me.

Were you looking for anything in particular?

I was looking for a snack.

What kind of snack?

Anything. I was just looking around. And then something in the freezer started melting.

I thought her eyes widened. They were dark, dark green.

What was melting?

I don't know. It was red.

Red? She looked away, toward the picture of Kurt.

There's nothing red in the freezer.

I don't know what it was, but it was red. I wiped it up. Then I went to look in the freezer.

What was it?

I didn't see anything.

She looked back at me. She smiled.

It was probably chocolate ice cream, she said.

She put a thoughtful expression on her face. Sometimes things that are brown look red.

I just looked at her. Her smile went away.

You were tired and dizzy.

Whatever, I said.

I tried to sit up, but she held her hands by my sides.

You should have something to eat, she said. Get that blood sugar back up. How about a bowl of ice cream?

She insisted that I stay in bed with a thermometer in my mouth while she went to the kitchen. She prepared me a bowl of vanilla ice cream. She told me that the container of chocolate ice cream had spilled all over the freezer. It had begun to melt and was dripping into the refrigerator. It was all taken care of, she said. She'd cleaned it up. She thought we should get a new fridge.

The ice cream slid into me like cold love. I felt it burn my tongue and the pink tissues along my throat. I listened to Pamela speak with the spoon in my mouth. I licked it backward and upside down, holding it in my mouth as if it were a lollipop. I was propped up in bed, listening to her speak. I didn't trust her, but in the strangest, saddest way, I felt safe. I felt uncertain but loved. Even scarier, I felt at home.

We should spend more time in the kitchen, Pamela said. I'd love to teach you how to cook.

I'd like that too, I said. I meant it.

Then she handed me some pills, and I took them.

3 2

IN DREAMS I OPEN MY MOUTH AND BUTTER-
flies come pouring out. But what happened wasn't a dream.
What happened was real. I opened my eyes and the shadows
took shape. They folded into origami wings. I opened my eyes
and I began to see.

I opened my eyes and out flew bats.

How can I get you to believe me? To believe the unbelievable?

If I tell you that it's happening all around you, will that
make a difference? Or will you think I'm just some psycho
teenage horror junkie?

*Here's our heroine, Beckett, a product of this culture, navigating
through it, and like everyone else she has to get by using what tools she
has. Ironically, these are the very tools of the culture: movies, fantasy,*

fiction. So she harnesses these forces in her own life, to live within the culture. Will she harness them for her own progress? Can she?

I see it everywhere, the thirst.

My father had called and Pamela had told him what had happened, so he'd picked up some magazines for me to read in bed. While the two of them ate dinner, I flipped through the magazines. The smooth paper felt like perfect skin. The deep colors like deep eyes. Women looked back at me from the slippery pages. But when I looked closer I noticed that they were looking past me, through me, at the posters on the walls. I imagined a world in which all of the pictures were looking at each other. The models staring at the posters which looked at the CD covers which were watching TV. Reflections of reflections.

I felt stuck in an infinite loop, where the only way out was to surrender and become another reflection. But I couldn't give up the hope that it might be possible to break free, to step outside. Then it occurred to me that I might have to step inside. I might have to step inside my nightmare, fight my battles, and only then come off the screen.

. . .

It doesn't matter whether something is real. What matters is whether it's true.

I fell asleep early. That must have been why I woke up in the middle of the night. I was wide awake and restless. I thought about trying Tobey at the hospital, but the night nurses got pissed when I called late. I got up and sat at my desk and turned on the computer.

The green glow on my face, an alien sun. I felt the cold warmth of it, a radioactive bath. I checked my e-mails and went to some of my favorite sites. The time started to slip into nothing as I scrolled down page after page into an eternity of words.

I'd just started to go into a Web trance when I found myself at a site about the occult, and horrifying organ music began piping out in weak audio. While that was playing, a graphic appeared on screen that looked like an etching of a wizard. It said it knew all kinds of folklore, and I could ask it any question. I kept pressing keys to move on and get away, but he kept insisting that I ask a question, and I got annoyed and typed in a question.

I asked about comas.

The wizard waved his wand, and pixels of dust swam around the screen. He looked more wizardly when he did that.

His beard jiggled a little, and his bony hand disappeared and reappeared in different places so that it looked like it was moving. Then the screen started flashing. It said: Do you believe? I typed in Yes, and it went on.

The wizard put down his wand and told me he would answer my question in due time, and that first he would have to educate me about the other world in general, and states of altered consciousness in particular, and that I could choose to skip this portion of the program if I wanted to, but that any effort to do so could interfere with the reliability of the information given as a result of the user not properly understanding it, and that this program was copyrighted and could not be reprinted or exhibited without prior written consent. I assumed they meant the wizard's consent.

Then the wizard went into his thing about comas. Trances, he said, are states that you can put yourself into with a little meditating or chanting. Visions require fasting, or maybe a pilgrimage or prayers. Then came a few more types of altered states. When he finished, all that he'd done was describe a bunch of things that I hadn't asked about. The wizard didn't seem to mind. Every time I tried to skip ahead, a message that said *All in Due Time* flashed on the screen.

After he'd proven how much he knew, the wizard waved his wand again, and said: So, do you want to hear what I have to say about blood? Before I could even answer, he started. He cited some ancient books that mention blood, and he described how blood moves through the veins. He told about methods of determining whether someone is inhabited by an evil spirit, and he gave recipes for potions that could remove the evil spirits. He gave a number you could call to purchase the potions. I tried to get out of the site.

All in Due Time flashed on the screen.

I wanted to turn off the computer, but a desperate feeling made me stay. I felt like I had nowhere else to go. It was a feeling I'd had before, only now it frightened me. I was just sitting there in my room, reading words on my computer, but I was scared.

The wizard said a few more things about blood, and then he asked me to be more specific in my question. He said to think very carefully about how I worded the question, because it was extremely important. I thought about it, and then I typed in specifically what I wanted to know.

You are interested in why people store blood.

Yes.

You wish to know why teenage girls die from loss of blood.

That is correct.

You really believe that the suicides were faked.

Yes, I typed.

Well, here's the whole truth, he said, and he started pixilating, and a drum roll played as he got ready to tell me. But

even before he said anything, I felt like I was one of those idiots in a movie who realizes the truth after everyone in the audience has known it for hours. I always hate that part. It gets
really boring at that point, while all the good guys figure things
out and tell each other and make plans. Sometimes they get it
wrong and there's a big twist later on. I never have much sympathy for them.

I turned off the computer, and the silence was so loud it was
like a subway train had driven through the room. I kept trying
to see my face in the blank screen. But all I could make out was
the corner of my eye. It kept twitching, like somebody had attached it to an electrical cord, and plugged it in.

33

IT WAS ONE OF THOSE BEAUTIFUL, MISERable days. I got out of bed and got dressed, and went to the kitchen. My father was sitting at the table, reading the newspaper. At first I couldn't think of anything to say. He didn't look up or look at me. My eye was still twitching.

Where's Pamela? I said.

She left already. He looked up. How do you feel this morning? He'd decided to play concerned dad.

All right.

How'd you sleep?

Okay.

I opened the refrigerator and looked around. There were no drips. I opened the freezer. It had been defrosted and neatened up. I pushed aside the frozen foods. The packages of tin foil were gone.

. . .

Rebecca, did you get any sleep last night? Were you on the Internet all night?

I wiped my eyes. Not all night.

You know, there's all kinds of crazy stuff out there. You can't just wander around out there and believe what you read. It's like walking out into the street and talking to just anybody. You wouldn't do that, would you?

He folded the newspaper. And then he folded it again. *He knows that she knows that he knows.*

Listen, you must be exhausted. He looked at me, and his eyes were clear. They were clear as glass.

Why don't you stay home today, he said. Get some rest.

No, I said. I feel okay. I want to go to school.

He looked at me, and finally he stood up and put the paper under his arm. Well, he said, that's nice to hear for a change.

He kissed me on the top of the head before he left.

After school, I didn't want to go home yet. I didn't want to go home without a plan, so I hung out to watch the band. They'd found a new guy since Tobey got sick. He was okay, but not half as good. I sat toward the back of the auditorium. I watched them set up their equipment, plugging things in and adjusting levels. Fuzzy noises and sudden squeals echoed while they got everything ready. They moved around on the stage like actors in a play; all their steps were so smooth and choreographed. I let my eyes get lost in the folds of their jeans, the way their cuffs softly grazed the tops of their flat sneakers. I imagined that I was the worn floor of the stage and that their gentle feet were walking all over me.

The music came down on me like sheets of colored rain. I sat there with my feet propped up on the seat in front of me, Tobey's wool scarf wrapped once around my neck, my long hair falling over my shoulders, my old jeans faded and smelling like Chinese food, my sweater scratching around my neck and wrists. For a moment I felt transported back to before things were so confusing, before I knew so much. I remembered lying on the bed in my room with Tobey, counting the shadows of the eyelashes that drew pencil marks on his cheek. I remembered the feeling of his weight against mine. I felt the bed sink underneath us.

When I open my eyes, the new guy is singing. He's holding the microphone close to his mouth, and the microphone stand is between his legs. He's pressing it up close to himself, his eyes closed, wailing something about the highway. I'm thinking, What does he know about the highway? He's just a city kid.

And then I notice that his pants are turning black. He's standing there, singing, and his jeans are turning black, right at his crotch, and the stain is getting bigger. Even from far away, I can tell what it is. Suddenly he stops singing:

Holy shit, the microphone screams.

I grabbed my coat and my book bag and headed down the aisle. When I got to the door to the auditorium, I looked down the hallway. I could see the back of Pamela's head. I could see her walking down the hall. She was wearing a crisp white shirt and dark blue jeans. Her long red hair was twisted up into a bun.

34

THE APARTMENT WAS EMPTY. I RAN TO MY room and turned on the computer. I went online and typed in the wizard's address. I waited. The elevator heaved. The buses choked. The radiator clanked like someone running a cup across the bars of a jail cell on TV. Then the computer told me I had been denied access to the wizard's Web site. I tried again, and was told I was too young. The computer said my parents were looking after my best interests, and a figure appeared who waved his finger from side to side like I should know better.

For a split second I see words from Dr. Kent's book:

The American teenager is in serious trouble, if not on the verge of extinction. Young people are killing each other and themselves. Where do we look for answers? To guns, to violent entertainment, to the In-

ternet, to the breakdown of the social fabric of society, to the "culture of narcissism," to ourselves?

I grabbed the phone and dialed.

Hello?

Tobey?

My heart drove off a bumpy road.

Who's this?

It's me.

Oh, baby.

We just hung there, breathing.

Are you okay?

I guess so, they sent me home.

I can't believe this. It's really you.

It's me. Oh, Beckett, I miss you.

I miss you too.

His voice echoed in my belly.

When can I see you?

I heard a click.

Hello? Tobey?

Hello, is this Beckett?

Yes.

This is Tobey's mother.

Oh. Hi, Mrs. Dillon. I'm so happy Tobey's better.

Yes. So are we. But he has to take it easy. And he can't be upset. He really has to get back to bed now.

Can I say good-bye?

I'm sorry, Beckett. I'm afraid not.

Then she hung up the phone.

The suitcase falls onto the bed. My clothes fly in. I go to the bathroom to get my things: soap, toothpaste, toothbrush. When I turn on the light, I look down. The little yellow wastebasket is empty.

I threw the stuff in my suitcase and closed it. I grabbed a printout from the computer and put it in my knapsack. I said goodbye to Kurt. I left the room.

Outside, I got on the bus. In the window, the city turned like channels. I closed my eyes. I thought about what Chloe had said about Venus. I thought about life on another planet, life on the other side of this screen, somewhere outside the movie.

The city looked back at me, a million broken images, the compounded eye of an insect. For a moment it all seemed frighteningly clear. Then suddenly, clouds moved overhead and a passing shadow darkened the streets, like a giant wing folding over the world. The city wrapping itself in twilight, getting ready to soar into night.

I realized, then, that even Venus wouldn't be far enough.

35

WHEN SHE OPENED THE DOOR SHE WAS WEAR-
ing a black jacket with a black shirt underneath and black pants.
I'd called before coming over, and she'd said it was okay, but she
only had a short time before her next patient. We took our
seats, but neither one of us had much to say for a few minutes.

You said you needed to see me, that it was very important.

I nodded.

You sounded very upset on the telephone.

I am upset.

Would you like to tell me why?

I looked up at her diploma, at the wrought-iron gates, and
past them into the garden.

It's very hard to talk about, I said.

She crossed and recrossed her legs.

. . .

Why don't you try, she said.

In the garden, a shadowy dusk. I wipe my hand across the sky and the color changes, like on a red velvet movie theater seat, only the sky isn't red, it's blue. It's dark blue in one direction, but when I wipe it with my hand, it gets lighter, a whitish soft gray blue, the color of the moon. The moon itself is up there too, full and silvery tonight, but still blending into the sky, not set off against the darkness. I watch the moon through the black branches of the trees. It looks like an egg in a nest.

When I finished telling her everything I knew, she leaned forward in her chair and looked me in the eye.

Beckett, she said, I think we're finally getting somewhere.

You're joking, right? I said.

No. She stood up and walked over to her desk. I thought she was going to bring me more pills, but she didn't. She was just sort of pacing around. She'd never done that before.

In Beckett's story, then, we see the suffering, the beauty, the mystery of the human mind. A girl with a vivid imagination, a father mourning a lost wife, and a woman trying to save them, set against a backdrop of cultural malaise and adolescent confusion——in Beckett's story

we see innocence twisted into the disease of our time, the disease of fan-
tasy, a disease created by a world in which there seems to be nothing
real.

Well, Beckett, she said, I think we're finally getting at your
deepest fantasies and fears.

I was back in the garden. The moon had finished rising.

You mean you don't believe me, I said.

Beckett, what matters here is not whether I believe you or
not, but how you perceive things. We're interested in uncov-
ering what's true for you.

This is true for me. What I've told you is true.

You think it's true that Pamela is trying to kill you.

Yes.

You think she wants your, as you said, menstrual blood.

Yes.

You think she and her fellow monsters, as you called them,
put a spell on virgins, a curse, you said, that makes the girls
bleed more than normal during their period.

Yes.

They give the girls potions and pills—or the curse can be
transmitted through animal fur. And though the girls get beautiful, eventually, you say, the girls hemorrhage and die. And
these monsters, or witches—you're not sure if they are
witches—whatever they are, they make it look like suicide.

Yes.

And you think that because Pamela needs the blood of a virgin, that she tried to kill Tobey so that you wouldn't sleep with him.

Yes.

I heard her eyes blink.

Beckett, these are very disturbing thoughts.

I didn't say anything.

You must be very frightened.

I closed my eyes.

You must feel very alone, with this knowledge and these fears.

When I opened my eyes, the moon was shining.

You must feel very powerful, to know these things and to be the subject of Pamela's interest.

I wipe my hand across the sky. It turns dark blue. The moon stands out. It hangs between the branches like a silver egg now, a magical glowing orb. I walk through the garden by the light of the moon. It's like the eerie light in a fish tank, only prettier. Little silver birds flit from tree to tree. Silver rabbits run out from behind bushes. I pick a silver flower, and it's heavy in my hand. The water in the lake gleams, like mercury.

Do you think that you're very important to Pamela, Beckett?

I don't know.

Do you feel, maybe, that you aren't as important to her since she married your father?

I don't know.

Do you feel less important to your father, since his remarriage?

All I know is that you don't believe me.

Everything that you think and feel is believed in here. But more important than believing is understanding.

She sat down again.

Beckett, she said, I think that your father's remarriage has been very difficult for you. I think that you felt Pamela was your friend, and then he took her away from you. And I think you felt that he was all yours, and now he belongs to her too. These feelings have stirred up all kinds of powerful associations in your mind, and you know, Beckett, you have a very active imagination.

I step into the lake, into the cool mercury. The silver surface rolls in slow, heavy folds. It slips around me like thick silk. It sticks to my arms as I swim through it.

I slide on my head underwater.

Beckett, she said from a million miles away, why do you think that Pamela wants to kill you?

I told you, I said, because that's what they do.

That's right, you told me. You said that "they" drink the menstrual blood of virgins until the virgins run out of blood and die. Why do you think, Beckett, that they would want to do that?

I told you.

Tell me again.

Because they want eternal life, eternal youth, beauty, whatever.

I see. Why?

Because they don't want to get old.

Are you afraid of getting old, Beckett? Would you like to stay a little girl?

Underwater, I see my reflection in front of me.

No, I don't, I said.

Why are you so sure that they want to be young?

Because they do.

How would the menstrual blood of virgins keep them young?

Look, I said, I can tell you don't believe me, so I should just leave, because I'm really scared.

That got her attention. She leaned forward again.

Beckett, she said, looking me straight in the eye, I'm concerned about you. I want you to think about a few things when you go home.

I don't want to go home. That's why I came here. I have nowhere else to go.

I don't want you to be alone, she said. She looked down at her hands. What about your friend's house?

Jen?

She looked up. Yes.

I felt a wave of relief. I would be safe at Jen's.

Why don't you go there?

She looked me in the eye again. She held my gaze, nodding.

Okay, I said.

She glanced at the clock. Our time is almost up.

She went on: I want you to consider your feelings about your father and Pamela and their getting married. I'd like you to think about what it means for you, this new relationship. I'd also like you to think about growing up, becoming a woman. Are you frightened by it? Would you like to stay a little girl? Do you think if you stayed a little girl forever your father wouldn't have married Pamela? I know that this is a lot to consider, but I'd like you to leave here with some new thoughts in your head, some ideas about how to think about all this.

I looked at my reflection under the silver water, and it looked back at me with tears in its eyes.

She seemed to almost reach out for me with her hand. Don't worry, she said. Everything's going to be all right.

I started to get my things together.

I wouldn't worry about vampires, she said.

. . .

Then she walked me to the door. I felt a tiny stab of air behind me as she closed it.

I'd never called them vampires.

I shoot up for air through the mercury pool. When I emerge,
the silver covers my skin. I am a statuette. I am like the figure
on the hood of a fancy car. My body gleams in the unearthly
moonlight. Then the silver begins to collect in little beads.
The beads drop off me like sweat. I am naked in the moonlight.
I am good. I am evil. I am running, and the mercury flies off
me and fans out behind me into wings of silver rain.

36

I TOOK A TAXI TO JEN'S HOUSE. THE DRIVER
tried to talk.

You are a very pretty girl, he said.

His cab smelled like sweet disinfectant and body odor.

Are you a model? he said.

Yes, I said. I'm a supermodel.

Ah-ha, he said. That's how I recognize you.

That must be it, I said.

Can I have your telephone number? he said.

Yes, I said. It's 911.

You're smart. I like smart girls, he said.

Could you take a kind of complicated route, maybe go up-
town a little too far and come back down?

Why? he asked.

Because I'm being followed.

You are a very exciting person, he said.

I had him drive me all over the Upper East Side, and through the park. He turned the meter off after I told him to go the long way. Driving through the city past the landmarks of my life, trying to avoid a predator, was like being inside my own video game. But the trees in the park weren't all the same shape. And the sky, it kept changing.

Finally, I had him drop me off in front of Jen's building. The doorman knew me and let me up.

How did I get into the apartment?

I don't remember.

Who was there?

Jen was there. And Chloe and Sofia.

What did I do when I saw them?

I don't remember that either.

37

AT NIGHT IN NEW YORK CITY, WHEN IT
starts to rain, the black umbrellas open, a million bats emerg-
ing from a cave.

The bats fly stealthily through the streets. They huddle in
doorways and slip into darkened theaters. Inside, they perch on
velvet seats. They look for themselves up on the screen. On
screen, the monster chases them through the maze. One by
one they die, but they don't care. They love the way their shadows look, so sexy.

But one person remains, one girl, the Final Girl. She out-
lives the others. She wields the knife.

She runs like a maniac across the screen. She has blood in
her hair and survival in her eyes. She stares hard at the monster. She's afraid of it, and then suddenly she's past being afraid.
That's when the Final Girl kills the monster. She stabs it, again

and again. When she's finished killing the monster, she slashes everything around her. Then she slices right through the screen. The Final Girl looks out through the gash in the screen, and she sees them, the bats looking hungrily up at her. She sees the silver dagger clenched in her hand, and just as she's about to let it go, she stabs herself in the heart. She feels the cold, silver dagger in her heart dissolve. She feels it morph into beads of mercury.

That's when she gets it. She gets the wisdom. And then she comes running off the screen.

38

THEY WERE ALL DEAD. I WAS THE ONLY
one left.

They'd done something awful with a pink plastic razor, two
of them on the bed and one on the floor. The music was still
lapping on the CD player. I think I mouthed the words.

When I close my eyes I can see them: Chloe, Sofia, and Jen.
They sprawl on the carpet, limbs dangling like stems. Their
heads are flowers. Their hair fans out in petals.

Chloe stretches. Sofia paints her nails. Jen reads. The time
is a liquid, and they swim inside it, moments collecting and dis-
persing like bubbles. They feel safe with each other. But at the
same time everything appears so quiet, so peaceful, an evolu-

tion is happening. The girls are growing. They grow like flowers, blooms shattering open in silence.

It's the growing that bothers the bats hiding in the hallway, the embodiments of greed, corruption, and fear. They hate the way the girls are beautiful and stupid, so free to be stupid, so young. They hate them and want to be just like them. They want to steal from them. Steal their beautiful youth and stupidity. And they want to catch it before it's too late, before the bloodred roses have opened and darkened, before all that beautiful, stupid girlhood is gone.

A society that sucks the life force out of individuals, especially children . . .

The bats hide in shadows. They imitate gargoyles on the facades of buildings. They pose like pigeons on the statues in the park. They blend into the shadows on the pavement, on pages. They slip between the covers of a magazine. When the glossy pages open, they unfurl with the sweet smells of perfume and glue. They dissolve into static and out of static, in the coffinlike interior of the television set. And on movie screens they glide in between the frames, in the black spaces between the frames. They slide across the screen like smoky clouds, and then they fly through the dust in the projector's beam and slip inside the holes of the audience's eyes.

. . .

She carried a black umbrella. She entered the apartment. She knew they would be there. She thought I would be there too.

The woman closed her umbrella, opened the front door, and stubbed out her cigarette with her shoe into the Tibetan carpet in the hall. Jen couldn't have heard these sounds because she was listening to the music on the CD player, but she felt something, a chill. Without looking up, she said to Chloe, What did you say? In the hallway, the woman leaned her black umbrella up against the wall. Chloe looked under her arm from inside her yoga pose and said that she hadn't said anything. I thought I heard something, Jen said. Sofia said that Jen was losing her mind. Jen put down her book, reached under her bed, and pulled out her secret box of pot. In the hallway, the woman took off her shoes. Jen rolled a joint and struck a match. As she struck it, she thought she heard the floor creak. As Jen took her first drag on the joint, the woman turned the knob on the door to the room. Jen stared at the knob. She watched it turn as she let out a stream of smoke. She saw it all unfold slowly before her. The door opening like a phantom door, the light through the glass doorknob splitting into prisms as the door opened, Sofia's head turning fast, a strand of her hair suspended for a moment, frozen, and the woman's black being entering the soft aura of the room, her hair flung across her face, across her sunglasses. Chloe rolled away backward, toward the bed, away from the woman. Sofia sat paralyzed, hands propped up behind her like a girl at the beach. The woman came at them without breaking her stride. Something metal glinted in her hand. Chloe climbed up onto the bed and grabbed Jen. Jen scrambled farther back, into the pillows. She saw the glint of metal move with a sense of direction, seeking them, looking for blood. She pulled the blankets up around her and Chloe as the woman bent down over Sofia and swung her arm. The metal splintered the air. It sliced low, right at Sofia's ankle. Sofia seemed surprised. She was still paralyzed, and then she grabbed for her ankle and the woman was on top of her, pinning her, and slitting her other ankle. She held Sofia's hands with one of her gloved hands, and she stuffed something into Sofia's mouth. Chloe and Jen huddled back into the wall. They held on to the blanket and squeezed each other. The woman slit Sofia's wrists. Jen grabbed her book and threw it at the woman. She grabbed another and another from her bedside table. The woman let them bounce off her coat. She stood up, and Sofia moaned over the music that was playing. The woman stepped over Sofia. The woman's face was cut, from her own blade, and scratched from Sofia's fingers, and her cheek began to bleed and the blood ran down like mascara. She came toward the bed. Jen could smell her. She came closer, and the blade winked in the air. It passed across the blanket. Chloe dropped the blanket and moved toward the end of the bed, away from Jen. The woman said nothing. Her movements were like a dance without sound, without feeling. Chloe's legs fumbled and kicked on the bed. Jen watched; she knew that the woman had come there to kill them, and she knew that who the woman really wanted was Beckett. Jen knew that the woman was angry that Beckett wasn't there, that she knew Jen was Beckett's closest friend, and it occurred to her that she was going to die in her own bed. She looked into the black holes of the woman's sunglasses and saw a terrible eternity, an eternity of anger.

Jen opened her mouth to an empty scream. The woman cut Chloe on her ankles and wrists. Jen felt the cold blade slice right through the blanket. She kicked and hit, and her hair thrashed like fire. Now Chloe was moaning over the music too. Jen jumped up and stood on the bed and contended with the woman, their arms locked, their hair igniting. The blade passed across her shirt. It searched for her wrist. The woman moved with inhuman speed, weaving the blade through the air. Their eyes met. Jen could make out something resembling eyes behind the dark glasses. Something like eyes, but they weren't eyes.

She made it look like a suicide. She planted the pink plastic razor. She arranged the bodies. When she finished, she wrote two words on the mirror. Two words in blood: DRINK ME.

part three

39

I RAN. I RAN AS FAST AS I COULD THROUGH
the park as the sun set.

I felt the bats all around me, in the shadows, in the trees. I felt
them watching me, following me, hunting me. They commu-
nicated with each other, too high for me to hear, but I felt the
sick electric vibration of their sound. As the darkness grew,
they unfolded from their hiding spots, spread their webbed
wings, and glided past.

The black umbrellas open along the streets as it begins to rain.
The umbrellas swoop around corners and slip into taxis. I run
through the park, down Fifth Avenue, past the museum. Any-

one looking would think I'm alone. But I am followed by a band of fallen angels flying behind me, squeaking and flapping in the night. When they fly in unison it looks like a plume of smoke, one black cape.

As I run I have a vision of her. She wasn't with the rest. She's celebrating. She's broken away and flown above the city. She soars over it all, circling the spires. She lifts her way up to the top of one of the tallest buildings, where she alights on a stone gargoyle. She folds her wings and tucks her head, and then, suddenly, she is a woman. She stands on the gargoyle, surveying the city, watching the black sky wrap the city in celluloid. The glossy night. The city like a flickering cold flame. She stands at the precipice and beholds her city. She spreads her wings. And then she dives back in to get me.

When I got to Tobey's, I sneaked into the apartment using the key that was always hidden in a plant. I walked down the hallway. His TV was on. Voices crying across time.

You know what happened next. I took off my T-shirt. I dropped it on the floor. Then I said: Fuck me.

He didn't want to. He was scared. I don't blame him. I was scary. I was soaking wet and panicked. He looked up at me like I was crazy. I hadn't seen him in weeks.

. . .

He reached his hands up toward me from the bed.

At first I pulled away, but then I moved close to him. I took off my wet jeans and tossed them on the floor. I got on the bed. I crawled under the covers.

I looked at him and brushed the wet hair out of my eyes.

You won't believe me.

Of course I will.

I took a deep breath and told him. I told him that they were after me, that they'd killed the beautiful girls, and now they'd killed Jen and Chloe and Sofia.

All he said was, Why?

Tears were racing down my face. I felt like someone had splashed me. I was already wet from the rain, but the tears were hot. They stung my lips.

Beckett, tell me.

Because I know about them.

What do you know?

I told him, that they needed my blood, that they only wanted virgins, that that's why he had to sleep with me.

I looked at him. It hadn't occurred to me how it would sound.

He looked so confused. I was worried that maybe he was still weak, or even sick, and that I was making it worse. He seemed not to know what to say.

Then suddenly he softened. I missed you, he said. He took my face in his hands.

We kissed gently for a minute, but then I pressed down on him and went at it harder. My tongue lashed in his mouth. I smashed my body into his. I straddled him and started to take off his underwear.

What are you doing?

I brushed my hair out of my face. I felt my cheeks flushed with blood. My raw lips.

I missed you too.

He grabbed my wrists. This isn't right, he said.

I couldn't explain to him what was happening. I couldn't tell him everything. I rolled next to him and put my head on his chest.

Climb up on board, he said.

The tears came back, only softer. I hooked my leg over his and he held me. For the first time in a long time, I felt calm. Calm, but not safe, and in an instant the feeling slipped away and I was running again, running through my mind.

I bolted up. I have to go, I said. They'll know that I've come here. She'll find me.

I climbed out of bed.

Beckett, get back in bed. I'm worried about you. You're not making sense. Have you been smoking anything? Have you been with Jen?

I reached down to the floor for my T-shirt.

. . .

When I stand up holding my T-shirt I turn around with my back to Tobey, facing the window. It is still dark, but I notice a movement out the window. The darkness is moving. Then I realize that the window is covered with bats. I see them shifting, shuffling, a living shadow. They are clinging to the ledge and to each other, watching me. I feel a numbing white whirlpool rush around in my head, and I go blank.

I must have fallen onto the bed and passed out. That's when the twister blew me away. That's when my insides hollowed out and spun around and someone sent me over the rainbow.

I woke up. The pillow was damp, and my hair was matted. There was a milky, purplish scrim of light between me and Tobey. He seemed to be made of static. I rolled over onto my side and faced the other way. I felt someone else in the room.

Hello? I whispered. I know you're here.

You're so smart, she hissed.

She was there.

40

IT WAS MORNING. I WAS ALONE IN THE BED.
It was drizzling outside and the sounds of Sunday-morning
cars skating along the avenue lifted into the room and I tried
to fall back to sleep, and then I remembered what had happened and where I was. I got out of bed and put on one of
Tobey's shirts and went and stood by the window.

Anything out there? someone said.

I turned around. It was Tobey.

It's raining, I said.

He had breakfast on a tray, like in a hotel. He'd even stuck
a flower in a glass.

Get back in bed, he said. I'll serve you.

I should get out of here.

You should have something to eat.

I got back under the covers. He placed the tray over my
legs. He sat on the edge of the bed and watched me eat.

You swallow so loudly, he said.

I laughed.

You do.

His hair was messy and spilling everywhere like a crazy salad. He smiled easily. I wasn't scaring him anymore. You were wild last night, he said.

We talked about things that had happened while he was in the hospital. I told him about my father getting married. I told him about the vision at school. I told him how real it had been. I didn't repeat the things I'd told him the night before, and he didn't ask. He told me about the hospital, the nurses, his room, but he didn't remember much of anything about the accident. He said they'd all been stoned and had the munchies and gone to the diner. He said he'd been pretty out of it. Then he said, I don't think my parents would be so happy if they knew you were here.

Why?

It's nothing to do with you, Beckett. They like you, he said. They're just really worried about me. They don't want me to get, you know, too excited.

He smiled and looked up at me from under his hair, and in a moment I remembered everything about him.

Do you still like ketchup? I said. I couldn't look in his eyes.

Yeah, he said. He lifted my face. I do.

My jeans were still wet, so I threw on an old pair of his shorts and left with the shirt of his I was wearing. It was still really early, so his parents weren't up yet. We walked quietly to the door, and in the hallway we waited for the elevator, and I held his hand. We started kissing in the elevator.

I can't go home, I said.

He nodded.

I'll call you when I know where I'm staying.

I wish you could stay here, he said. But my parents . . .

It's okay.

We were hugging when we got to the lobby and the elevator doors opened. I looked up and saw the little convex mirror in the upper corner of the wood-paneled elevator. In it was the reflection of a figure standing just outside the door. It was Dr. Kent.

I pulled away from Tobey and pressed all the buttons in the elevator, but he blocked my hands and dragged me out into the lobby.

My fingernails scraped against the wood paneling in the elevator. My fingers clutched his flannel shirt.

He held me tightly around the arm, and I turned to look at him. He looked the same. He looked like he loved me.

How could you do this? I said.

I'm worried about you, Beckett. You seem out of control.

I tried to pull away, but he held on. My damp sneakers skidded across the marble floor.

· · ·

The lobby was cool and dark and long and narrow. Dr. Kent had been waiting inside, not far from the elevator, but when she'd seen us she'd started walking quickly out to the street. Now, as we approached the front door—the drizzle was still hanging like a veil—I could see her standing outside a waiting taxi. The door was open, and I could see the empty seat.

You don't understand, I was crying, she's with them.

Beckett, he was pulling me with both arms now, you need some help, and I love you. I couldn't reach your father, and I thought of Dr. Kent. I mean, I know how much she's helped you.

I was sobbing as they put me in the taxi. Dr. Kent closed the door and stood on the sidewalk, under the apartment building's awning, talking to Tobey. Tobey listened to her and nodded a couple of times. From the darkness of the lobby, the doorman stood, watching us.

I could see Tobey through the smudged window. He looked worried about me, running his hand through his hair. But then his expression changed. It was like he remembered something. He looked back at me through the window, and I knew from his look that he believed me, if only for a split second. And then it was gone and he waved good-bye as if he'd never see me again.

Dr. Kent opened the heavy cab door and slid in beside me. She was carrying a black umbrella.

4 1

I TRIED TO BOLT OUT MY SIDE OF THE taxi before it started, but the door was locked from up front, like a police car. I could only see the back of the driver's head through the partition in front of me, but it was a woman. Dr. Kent leaned over and fastened my seat belt, like some kind of demonic flight attendant. The belt didn't just flip closed; it had a lock. Dr. Kent put the key in her purse. When I was all strapped in, with my hands strapped as well, she took out a silver pillbox, took out two blue pills, and put them in my mouth.

Swallow them. They'll calm you down, she said.

I spit them out.

Suit yourself, she said. Then she took out two more pills and rammed them down my throat. I gagged, but she forced a bottle of water in my mouth and made me swallow.

She sat back and sighed. She took a sip from a paper coffee cup. It had the old-fashioned I Love New York logo emblazoned on it in red.

I stared out the window. The drizzle wept.

There was no garden anymore. No iron gates. I had escaped the garden, I was running now, but it seemed that the gates had only led me into a vast, sprawling cemetery. I'd thought that when I ran I would be running through a beautiful forest, a valley, along a river. But I seemed caught in a graveyard that spread on for miles, and behind every stone lurked a moving shadow.

The taxi pulled up at Dr. Kent's office. She leaned toward me and unlocked my seat belt and dragged me out into the street. My head swam. She grabbed my arm and ushered me into the building, then into the waiting room where I had waited so many times before.

She sat me down and locked the door. Then she went into her office and disappeared into a side room. My eyelids were half closed. She must have thought I was out already. But I pulled myself up. I walked over to the receptionist's area.

I sat behind the counterlike desk. There were files behind me. A phone, a Rolodex, a cup of pens. And a big computer. It was easy to turn on. My eyes kept rolling back into my head, but my fingers found the keyboard. I went online. I found him. He was still there.

. . .

He materialized on screen with a twangy jingle, like techno ice-skating-rink music. He was wearing his ridiculous wizard hat and holding his wand in one hand. In the other he gripped a cigarette.

What can I do for you? he asked.

HELP, I typed over and over.

All right, he said. I get the picture.

He walked toward me, his skinny, pixilated body disintegrating and reforming with each step.

Ask me questions, he instructed.

It's not just Dr. Kent, is it? I typed.

No, he said. She's just one of them.

How can I get away?

You can't, he said.

Not ever????

Not yet. Be patient.

My eyes rolled back again. My head sank to one side. Out of the corner of my eye I saw him walk even closer. He was knocking from the inside of the screen.

Hey, kid, he said. Wake up. There's not much time.

I ripped open my eyes and typed: Help help help help help.

What do you think? he said. I'm going to ask for the umbrella of the wicked witch of the West? This ain't fairy tales, kid.

You suck, I said.

Okay, okay, he said. Remember this. Then he took a drag on his cigarette and coughed. He kept coughing.

Are you okay? I typed.

Remember this. He stubbed out his cigarette and made a silly motion with his hand, and struck a wizardly pose: Everyone has their shortcomings.

Yes? I typed. Is that all?

Think about it.

Thanks a lot.

Everyone has their shortcomings, he said. And hers is being evil. Think about it.

Fuck you, I typed.

Watch your language, he said.

You fucking useless piece of nothing, I typed.

He lit another cigarette. The flame looked bright pink.

Don't curse, he said. And with that he dissolved off the screen.

42

WHEN I WOKE UP IN THE BACKSEAT OF THE
taxi, I had the feeling that I was a passenger on a train of my
own thoughts, a voyager in my own dark dream.

What matters isn't whether something is real. What matters
is if it is true.

The motion of the car was like a speeding heart. I was lying
down, strapped like clothes inside fancy luggage. I turned my
head. I tried to move my arms. I listened but I couldn't make
out anything, just a muffled, meaningless sound coming from
the front seat. My head ached, and the smell of the taxi shoved
up my nose like a poison. After a while I got used to the slick,
filthy feel of the vinyl seat. I rested my head and listened.

Hello? I whispered. Hello? She was there. I could feel her.
Hello? No one answered.

But there was something, someone, traveling with me. It was
the same presence I'd felt in Tobey's room. The same demon
who spoke to me in my dreams. She was there. I could hear her
breathing. Then I heard the voice that I'd heard before: *You
should kill yourself.*

I started to wonder if it wasn't a good idea. I seemed to
have lost all sense of reality, and I felt myself hurtling closer to
an emptiness inside that threatened to take over. And then it
did just that. I'd been fighting it for so long, it seemed the only
way to live, but all at once, in the taxi, I let it take over. I felt
it. I felt the cold mechanical loneliness of my deepest self, and
I realized that I didn't need to kill myself. I was dead.

Then I thought about what the wizard had said: *Everyone has
their shortcomings.* My shortcoming, I thought, is that I had already died. I thought I'd come back to life when I'd found
beauty and friends and love, but I hadn't. It was a false life. If
I wanted a real one, I understood, I would have to fight for it.

There was no one to save me: not Dr. Kent, not Tobey, not my
father, not the wizard.

When Persephone went down to Hell, her mother followed. But I didn't have a mother. There was no one coming
after me.

43

THE WHITE BUILDING WAS UP AHEAD, SHIV-
ering in the windshield. The most unassuming spot, the most
dangerous place. A tall wall of windows. A face with nothing
but eyes.

When the door opened there was a blinding light, and I could
see that the rain had stopped. I looked up at Dr. Kent from
below and she seemed a thousand feet tall, like a monster in a
silent movie, a cheap special effect. She leaned over me in her
tight clothes and high heels and unstrapped me from the seat.
I recognized her perfume. It was the same kind Pamela had
given me.

We were pulled up in front of the white-brick building. At
first I thought I was having déjà vu or that I'd been placed in

some familiar dream, but then I realized that I really had been there before. It was the building Pamela had lived in when I first met her. It was the most boring, nondescript building in the world.

Dr. Kent dragged me into the lobby. I remembered the lobby: shabby, with a vaguely seedy doorman standing behind an ugly desk. A middle-aged woman with a scrappy dog on a leash leaned against the desk, talking to him. I had the feeling she was always there. People walked through the lobby: a typical mix of weary people. It was as if the building drained the life out of them, this unglamorous, ugly building on a busy corner, where the subway vibration sent a deadly shiver through the pipes, and the fumes from the cars and buses turned the white bricks gray and then brown over the years. This building seemed to hold within it everything sad and lonely and aspiring and pathetic about the city. Still, it was hard to imagine anything really sinister going on in there. It looked so bland.

As Dr. Kent pulled me toward the elevator, we passed a row of mailboxes. I caught a glimpse of Pamela's box. On the box, her name was printed in white letters against black, only it was spelled differently from the way she spelled it at school and with us. It was spelled *Pam Rive.* As we moved past the mailbox, I stared at the letters, and they rearranged themselves before my eyes. It might have been funny if I hadn't been terrified.

44

THE TWENTIETH FLOOR LOOKED JUST LIKE any other. It was long and carpeted and dimly lit, with faded sunflower wallpaper. Every door was shut.

Dr. Kent grabbed my arm and pulled me down the hall. She straightened her hair before ringing the bell.

A woman opened the door. She looked like a typical mother from my school except that she was carrying a book. In the background I could hear a group of women talking. Dr. Kent asked if Pamela was there. I'll get her, the woman said.

A few seconds later, Pamela appeared on the threshold, the door open just enough to let her through. She was also carrying a book. Her fingers curled around its spine.

Hello, Beckett, she said. She leaned against the doorway, her long body curving against the straight wall.

She smiled as if she were trying to calm me down. Beckett,

she said, we're all very concerned. Dr. Kent called and asked if she could bring you here. We're in the middle of a book group, but I always have time for you.

I kept feeling myself moving in and out of reality. I must have looked confused because then Pamela said, Are you wondering why I still have this apartment? I believe in keeping a room of one's own.

You're lying, I said.

Pamela looked at me, deeply concerned.

I know you killed my friends, I said.

She looked at Dr. Kent and said: Now she's hallucinating.

Dr. Kent nodded. It's to be expected, she said. Don't respond.

Beckett, have you done anything, anything dangerous? Pamela asked. She gave Dr. Kent a worried look.

You can trust us, Dr. Kent said.

They looked perfectly normal.

Why don't you come inside? Pamela said.

I saw a tiny smudge of red in the corner of her mouth that looked like lipstick.

Because you're going to kill me, I thought.

Beckett, Pamela said, I love you. I'll understand whatever you've done.

That's when I started screaming.

45

THEY DRAGGED ME INTO THE APARTMENT. Inside the apartment were about fifteen women. They were standing around the living room, which looked the same as when I had visited with my father. Some of the women I recognized—they were the mothers of kids from school, or other teachers. Some of them I'd met at my father's wedding. Some I recognized from my dreams. They were just standing around, nothing scary. They were all drinking tea.

No one was reading a book. Every single one of them was holding a white china teacup with a little handle in the shape of a tiny *c* and a matching white saucer. They all stopped sipping, suddenly, when I came into the room.

Should I call the hospital? Dr. Kent said.

No, please, not yet, Pamela said.

. . .

Pamela lit a cigarette. Her hands were steady, but when she went to take a puff, I saw that her lips were trembling. I couldn't tell if it was for real.

Dr. Kent pushed me down onto the couch, and Pamela sat down next to me. She took a deep breath. Beckett, she said, we know that you are a brilliant girl, with a wonderful, active mind. We can only imagine what kinds of thoughts and dreams, and nightmares, you've been having. Here she paused and wiped away a tear.

We can only imagine, she repeated. What upsets us, she said, is the thought that you have in any way acted on these fantasies of yours. She took a long drag and stared at Dr. Kent.

Dr. Kent nodded and said: The deaths of Sunday, Morgan, and Myrrh seem to have sparked your imagination in a treacherous way.

But we're afraid, Pamela said, that we can't hide anymore from the idea that you have done something. Something terrible. All these violent and outrageous thoughts you've been having, we're worried that they've led you to hurt people. Beckett . . .

Tears were pooling in her eyes now, like water over stones in an icy stream.

Did you hurt Tobey because you were afraid he didn't love you? Did you hurt Chloe and Sofia and Jen?

The tears were snaking down her neck.

Did you?

I was silent. All around me, images were spinning, like tiny television sets floating in space. I saw the first time I met the nurse, in her office, with Tobey there. I saw myself discovering the bodies of the three dead girls. I saw Tobey in my arms. I saw my face in the mirror. I saw blood in my hair, on my face, on my lips. I didn't know what was real or imagined anymore. And the women just stood there sipping tea.

I couldn't stop looking at the teacups. Each one had a string hanging over the side, from the tea bag. But there was no little paper tab with a saying on it attached to the string.

Suddenly I knew what was inside the teacups. The tea was made from blood.

46

A LOUD WHOOSH MOVED THROUGH MY SKULL, and my body felt empty, as if my head had detached from it and everything had flown away. It was obvious to me what was happening: I was seeing the truth, like a streak of color through a rip in a black-and-white movie screen.

I must have passed out. When I woke up, I was in Pamela's bedroom. I remembered the bedroom from that time long ago in Pamela's apartment, when I'd sat on the bed watching television while my father and Pamela flirted in the living room. Their voices came back to me, the way they had floated in and out of the television sounds like another show while I snooped around in Pamela's closet, trying on her sexy high-heeled shoes and fingering through her scarves. I remembered feeling so far away from them, eavesdropping on their conversation, with its adult nuances and loaded silences, which at the time seemed so meaningful and filled with possibilities, threatening and exciting. But now the charade of it all was laid bare. I saw how stupid I had been.

I could hear Pamela talking to the women in the living room. Her voice was different now, more authoritative. I went to the door, but it was locked. I sat at her desk, turned on the computer, and went online.

The wizard was in. He morphed on screen like static making sense, pulling himself together and picking up his wand.

HELP ME, I typed.

I know, I know, he said. Always in trouble.

He retreated a few steps, dissolving and recombining like smoke.

TELL ME WHAT TO DO.

The orange teardrop shape of a flame appeared as he struck a match twice his size.

How do I know, kid? he said.

WHAT DO YOU MEAN?

He took a long drag on his cigarette.

You've got to think on your feet now.

BUT I THOUGHT YOU KNEW WHAT TO DO.

Stop shouting. You're giving me a headache.

I unwrapped a piece of chewing gum.

The wizard blew smoke rings. He tilted his head, like he was thinking.

Now you're on to something, he said.

CHEW GUM? I typed.

Swallow it. Take in the life force, he said. The power of nature.

IT'S GUM, I typed.

You're ingesting the sap of the tree, he said.

WHAT TREE?

The tree of knowledge. The tree of life. The one true way. Living, dying, eating, regeneration. It's the cycle, you can't fight it.

I DON'T UNDERSTAND.

Think about it.

HELP ME, I typed over and over.

You're a smart person, he said. You can figure it out.

His cheesy theme jingle played as he disappeared. "Check out links to other occult sites" flashed on and off.

I took out the gum and stuck it on the back of the computer.

47

OUTSIDE, I HEARD MY FATHER'S VOICE. ITS deep mystery, its sad cadences. He was talking to the women; then I heard his footsteps, and the door to the bedroom opened. I turned around in my chair. He peered in.

He looked at me, and his eyes let go of everything. His eyes, which had held back so much for so long, they emptied right in front of me, like two windows that had been shut and now shattered. I knew then that he had known about her, maybe not all of it, but enough to make a choice. But I also saw that he had done it for me. He'd gone to her for me, so that I could have a mother. And he'd gone to her for himself, to protect me from his loneliness and need. But he hadn't protected either one of us.

I recognized that something inside me was changing because I didn't blame myself for everything that had happened when I saw my father. And I didn't blame him. I saw past blame, as if it were only a reflection. I just saw him.

He looked at me, and nodded, then closed the door gently like a kiss.

I heard the door shut, and I heard him say: she's fine. Then he said good-bye to the group and to Pamela, and the front door closed behind him.

He'd left the door to Pamela's room unlocked. He was telling me to escape.

Sometimes I think about my life, and movies, and this beautiful stupid country we live in, and I think that I don't know which is which. But I'm trying to tell the difference. I'm trying to see through all that phony emotion into the heart of things, into my own heart. In the video of the movie of my life on this planet, my heart at the moment when I get up from the desk to open the door is a speck of color, an orange point of light. But watch it explode. Watch it splatter. Watch it atomize, metastasize, and burn.

48

IT WAS A MAD TEA PARTY. THE ENTIRE ROOM
seemed transformed, cockeyed, as if lit by a neon moon. What
had been tame and subdued before sprang into color, height-
ened, saturated, steeped. The women's faces were flushed and
giddy, and their eyes were glowing. Revelers at a midnight
clearing in an artificial forest.

When I opened the door I was on the other side, over the rainbow, down the rabbit hole, into the woods.

I tried to run past them, to the front door, but they blocked the
way. I was trapped in the living room.

    Pamela emerged from the kitchen. She had put on fresh

makeup and changed her clothes. She had on a short trench coat over a silk shirt and skirt, and high heels. Her eyebrows looked dark and fierce. She paced back and forth in front of me. The living room wasn't very big, and the ceilings were low. She seemed caged. She seemed enormous.

Please, I said. Don't hurt me.

Why would I want to hurt you? she said. I'm not your mother.

It seemed like the statement of a lunatic. What do you mean? I tried to say. But the words stuck in my throat and I began to cry. I cried because I thought of another meaning. I thought, Maybe she understands me, understands that my mother hurt me when she died. Maybe she really does love me.

Then, like a convulsion, the sobs overtook me. I saw Pamela's face grimace in sympathy. She reached out her arms to me, but first she looked toward Dr. Kent, as if to ask, Is it all right? Dr. Kent nodded.

Pamela leaned forward and put her arms around me. I fell into them, longing for comfort. She held me tightly. My wet face nestled against her breast. I felt the rough silk of her shirt, the damp of her chest, the wetness on her neck from her own tears. She rocked the two of us back and forth for a little while, saying soothing words into my hair. I smelled the cigarette smell on her breath and clothes. I smelled my father on her skin. I smelled her perfume. It felt familiar, and I breathed it in deeply.

I tilted my face to look up at hers. It was my mother's face. It was my mother.

Oh, Beckett, she whispered.

She held me closer, her arms wrapped around me like the limbs of a tree. I remembered a tree, weeping, at her funeral. I remembered her touch. I reached for her hand and took it in mine. It was my mother's hand, the skeleton of a tiny kitten.

She looked in my eyes, and I saw my reflection in the silver pond.

Tears welled up in her eyes, my mother's eyes, and she let them roll down her cheeks. Outside, a siren wailed and drifted off. A bus pulled up at the corner. It occurred to me that I hadn't heard these noises before and that I was hearing them now only because it was completely quiet. The women were silent.

Suddenly I noticed that my mother's touch had changed. Her arms were tense. Her neck stiffened. I felt her face rummaging around in my hair, as if she were looking for something.

Then I realized what she was doing. She was sniffing. She was sniffing me as if I had a bad smell.

I looked around the room, at the frozen assembly. My mother followed my gaze and turned around. She seemed to turn in slow motion. First her eyes disappeared, then her skin, then all I could see was her hair.

When she turned back, she was no longer my mother. Her eyes were red with rage.

She let go of our embrace and pushed me away, gently, containing her anger. Deep in thought, she looked through me, as if I had disappeared.

She reached into her leather bag and got another cigarette. She lit it. She crossed her legs and took off one shoe. She put the high-heeled shoe in her lap and massaged her foot with one hand while she kept the cigarette in the other. She took a long drag and stared off into space.

She shook her head. She took another puff.

Damnation, she said.

Then she smiled, just a little, to herself.

It was when she said that that I noticed Dr. Kent. She was shaking.

Pamela looked up at her.

You useless piece of shit, she said quietly.

What are you talking about? Dr. Kent mouthed, but nothing seemed to come out.

You let the girl out of your sight, didn't you? You idiot. She's had sex.

Dr. Kent looked at me. Is this true? she said. If it is, this is very upsetting. Sex brings on strong feelings, feelings that might be difficult for you to manage. Not to mention that you're very young, Beckett. Pamela is concerned for your welfare, and so am I.

No you aren't, I whispered.

Beckett, having sex might make you feel like a woman, and it might be a way for you to master the strong emotions stirred up by your mother's death, a way to assert yourself, but it is not a good idea. All your rage, your fantasies . . .

Shut up, Pamela said.

I'm sorry, Dr. Kent mouthed.

Don't be sorry, Pamela said. Be scared out of your fucking random mind.

That's when Dr. Kent collapsed onto the floor in front of me. She crumpled in fear, one leg shaking spasmodically. Her hand reached out to steady it. The only noise in the room was the sound of her shoe bouncing against the floor. None of the tea-drinking women moved. They stood there, like an audience frozen in suspense, cups lifted halfway to their lips.

Pamela took a last drag on her cigarette and threw it on the floor, and stubbed it out with her bare foot. Then she took the shoe that was in her lap; she grabbed it by the middle and she drove the heel of it into Dr. Kent's eye, like a spike.

Behind the high-pitched miserable anguish of Dr. Kent's wail, I heard the teacups shivering in their saucers.

I felt betrayed by Dr. Kent. I had trusted her, and I needed her. I think that she really did want to help me. Maybe once upon a time she was a good person and had wanted to help people, but even if she had wanted to help me she couldn't have. Not really. I had to help myself.

Get rid of this, Pamela said.

No one moved.

Why am I waiting? she said.

A teacup shattered on the floor. Two women came forward and lifted Dr. Kent's body and took her away.

Pamela wiped her shoe on the bottom of the couch. Then she put it back on. She turned to me. She seemed perfectly normal.

So, Beckett, how was it?

I opened my mouth to scream, but nothing came out.

How was Tobey? You can tell me.

49

WHY DIDN'T I TELL YOU THAT I SLEPT WITH Tobey? Because that was private. That was more private than the gated garden. That was a dream for him and me.

Persephone, Dorothy, Lolita, the Final Girl: I'm following you. I'm on my way.

5 o

HER EYES FLASHED. HER SKIN WAS DAMP.
Her hair stuck to her brow.

Did you think having sex would save you? she said. Because
it won't.

Then she said she wanted a cup of tea before she said
good-bye.

Bring me Beckett's drink.

A woman appeared from the kitchen carrying a white
teacup. The little white string hung over the side. Pamela sat
down on a chair opposite me. She pushed her hair away from
her face. She crossed her legs.

The women were looking at her, mesmerized. I noticed
their faces, like masks, and their beady eyes behind them,

ancient with unhappiness and hidden amid a false, young skin.

As the woman handed Pamela the teacup, I thought about what it would be like to die. I realized that after Pamela finished the blood, she would kill me, like she'd killed the others. I thought about everything I had already lost: my mother, my father, even Tobey, now, because he would never believe I hadn't lost my mind. I had nothing, I thought. But then I remembered what the wizard had said about the life force, and I felt the freedom of having nothing, no one, and I sensed myself a little bit alive. I was back in the garden, only now the gates were open wide, and outside there was a world. The life force, I thought. The cycle of living and dying. I knew what I had to do.

Here's our heroine, Beckett. Will she harness the forces of evil for her own progress? Can she?

As she lifted the cup to her lips I felt an energy surge through me and rip past everything that had held me down.

I grabbed the cup from her hand. I drank the blood. I drank my own blood in a single shot.

5 1

THE WOMEN SHRIEKED. PAMELA STOOD THERE, very still.

I felt the blood course through me. It was hot and cold at the same time, fiery and silver. I grabbed Pamela by the hair, and she pulled away, but I had her.

The women rushed toward me, but Pamela motioned for them to stay back.

She knelt down in front of me.

Her mascara was all smeary, and her lipstick was bleeding into tiny cracks. Her eyes were enormous, and they stared sideways at me, demented and desperate. They darted away, seeking pity, then slinked back with the timing of a silent-screen star.

She started to cry and I almost felt something. But I could see her now, her tricks, her schemes. She was everything empty: money without value, youth without hope. She was beauty without meaning.

Let me tell you what it was like. It was like an X ray of a horror movie.

Suddenly she lunged toward me, knocking me down. Her arm like a wing coming toward my eyes. Her hand groping in midair with the fingers splayed like claws and the painted nails flashing and her thick hair shaking wildly like a hundred snakes. Her movements were no longer human. She flung her arm across my face, and I landed on the couch. She pulled me down onto the floor. I saw the floor closely, the creases in the fake grain, the thick varnish. I heard the bus pull away outside, and that's when I saw her teeth for the first time, glinting behind her red lips. They were pointed like knives, and they sought me out as if they had a mind. I jumped up, scrambling against the floor and the couch. She stood up after me and pushed me into a bookshelf. Then she knocked the entire shelf out of the way. Oversized occult books tumbled onto the bare floor, and she tripped on one of them as she reached out for me again, hitting her head against the wall and a tiny trickle of blood like a narrow road on a map formed on her forehead. I could smell the strange smell of her blood. It smelled like dead flowers and wine and burning meat. I tried to make my way past her but she kept coming at me and I kept ducking. Finally she grabbed me by the shoulders. The side of my face hit the wall. I tasted a raw sore taste in my mouth. It occurred to me that I would die here, in this unremarkable apartment, with the city sounds masking my screams. I looked into her eyes, and then she lifted me again and threw me beyond the door of the bedroom. She was all teeth now, and wings like weapons. Three women had been sitting in the bedroom, and they stood up slowly in unison and headed back into the corridor. One didn't make it and she stood silently by the window. Pamela's face came down upon me, and her teeth slashed through my shirt. She was moving like an animal now, her body swaying, her mouth dripping. I was watching her eyes, watching for the end. They were eyes that were so familiar with death they would alert me with their sense of impending satisfaction.

Then I flew. She had lifted me and in one motion picked me off the bed and thrown me across the room, against the opposite wall. There was a mirror on the wall. I saw myself flying toward it. Time stopped for me. I saw the room pressing back at me, doubling forward. The woman standing silently by the window, eyes wide, enlarging as the mirror closed in on me. The bed vaulting through space, flat and distorted against the wall. Pamela's figure growing smaller and more enormous at the same time, hurtling at me and away, my own shape slicing through hers, as I hit the glass, cracked the glass, traveled through time.

I saw my bloodied face, and behind that my new, beautiful face, and behind that the face I used to wear, my lonely face. I saw them merge together into a face I had never seen. A face that looked back at itself, a face that was not a mask.

And as the face became my own it broke into a thousand

faces and I landed on top of the dresser, pieces of silver falling around me like mercuric rain. She was there. She was standing above me and took hold of my hair by the roots and forced my face back to bite my neck. As she did so I brought a piece of broken mirror up from the dresser, held it high in the air like a sword, like a torch, and sank it into her heart. I ripped through her heart and I pulled out the mirror and lifted the blood-streaked mirror in front of her face.

Pamela's eyes stared into the mirror. The blood flowered across her torn white silk shirt but she did nothing to stop it or reveal that she was in pain. She took the mirror from me. She stared at her reflection and dropped the mirror. It shattered on the floor. Then the school nurse leaned forward and fell like the mirror, shattered in silver rain, and disappeared.

The women had crowded into the room. Now they filed out, like patrons leaving a movie theater, crying sentimental tears.

I brought myself down from the dresser, slowly. No one helped me. I walked gingerly, barely holding myself up. Blood coated my hair. My limbs were numb. I had bits of glass in my skin. I felt dazed but strangely calm. My hands were swollen and cut, and my eyes had trouble focusing.

I was standing when one of them came up to me and spoke. I recoiled, but turned to face her.

Don't touch me, I said.

Can we help you? Are you hurt?

Leave me alone.

Her voice was high, sputtery. It gurgled the words. We'll go now, she said.

As I turned to leave the room my body gave out underneath me. The room twisted and turned. Outside, the traffic was tuning up like an orchestra. The wail of horns and violins. I was lying on the floor. Someone leaned over me, a passing shadow. It was Tobey. He gathered me in his arms and held me close and carried me through the apartment and out the door and took me away as night was falling and the lights arrived and music sounded.

5 2

WHEN I WOKE UP IN THE BACKSEAT OF THE
taxi, I had the feeling that I was a passenger on a train of my
own thoughts, a voyager in my own dark dream.

But this time I wasn't alone. Tobey was holding my hand.

That look he'd had on his face, remembering something. I
know now he believed in me. He came after me.

How can I get you to believe me? To believe the unbelievable?
Maybe I can't. Maybe you won't. But I don't need you to believe me. I believe in myself.

.   .   .

My father's been away for a while now, back out on the island. He's figuring out who he is again, without my mother, without anyone.

And I'm figuring out who I am without my mother. I know now she didn't want to hurt me. She didn't want to die. I hear her voice sometimes, a shaky lullaby. But I don't hear sirens anymore.

I rent a room in an apartment where another family lives. It's not far from school. I spend most of my time with Tobey. Sometimes, when he's asleep, I sit by myself in the bathroom. I look at myself in the mirror and see all my selves, past, present, and future. I see my face explode into a million shards. Then I see her bloody reflection splinter into a prism of terror, and I'm back inside the kaleidoscope.

That's when I open the medicine cabinet. I reach for the colored pills. I kept some. They remind me of my old self, of temptation, of not trusting that I can be enough.

I look at my tearstained face in the mirror. I pour two pills in my hand. Then I look into my eyes and see not my mother's eyes or my father's eyes but my own eyes. I look at myself and look back at myself. I'm beginning to see who I am. Then I put the pills on my tongue to remind myself how close danger is. But I don't take them.

. . .

Yesterday, on my way to school, I saw a barren tree filled with bats. It scared me, but when I got closer, I saw that it was only a torn umbrella caught in the tangled branches.

Today I saw a rainbow. It stretched from the river to Central Park. It was a perfect rainbow, fruit-punch colors against a late-spring sky, an archway over the city. No one was looking up at it.

I don't understand why nobody notices. Those rainbows, they turn Manhattan into heaven.

Persephone, Dorothy, Lolita, The Final Girl: I drank my blood and found a voice inside me deeper than pain. I looked in the mirror and found a face beyond beauty. I walked up on screen into a vision that was terrifying and true. And when I came back I was more innocent than before. The world was glimmering and strange.

I sat under a tree. The leaves waved down to me. The light burst through them, butterflies on fire. I wished that everyone could feel how I felt now: alive and free. So I wrote down what had happened. I wrote it in blood. You can say you don't believe me. You can say that I'm crazy. But I've been places I could never have dreamed of. And you were there. And you, and you, and you.

JANE MENDELSOHN's first novel, *I Was Amelia Earhart*, was a national bestseller and has been published in fifteen languages. She lives in New York City with her husband and daughter.